PRAISE FOR TAMARA

"A relentlessly fun revenge story AND a gut-wrenching exposé of the murky currents of high school sociology. Jeffrey and J.D. masterfully weave a tale of revenge and terror."

- Stephen Susco, screenwriter, The Grudge, The Grudge 2 & Texas Chainsaw 3D.

"Tamara is relentlessly paced, gory as hell, and packs a plot-twist so sharp, it'll leave a scar. This is Jeffrey Reddick at his diabolical best!"

– J.C. Hutchins, author of The 33, the 7th Son Trilogy & Personal Effects: Dark Art

"A triumph from screen to page, Tamara shines as a horror novella with vivid characters, writing that flows, and plenty of chills and thrills!"

– Stephen Zimmer, author of the Hellscapes and Rising Dawn Saga.

"Darker, sexier, bloodier... this is the definitive telling of Tamara's terrifying tale. The story, crafted with J.D. Matthews, shows that Jeffrey Reddick is as much a force to be reckoned with on the page as he is on the screen. A MUST READ for horror fans!"

– Steve "Uncle Creepy" Barton - Dreadcentral.com

TAMARA

Jeffrey Reddick and J.D. Matthews

Piper Press 69
960 North Alfred Street
Suite 209
West Hollywood, CA 90069
https://www.facebook.com/Tamarathenovel

ISBN: 978-0692329054

1.   Supernatural - Fiction. 2. Horror. 3. Thriller 4. Teen. 5. Young Adult (YA) 6. Final
            Destination 7. Film adaptation.

Library of Congress Control Number: 207 5489001

Printed in the United States of America

Chapter 1

"He's going to want me," she said, the words escaping her mouth like cigarette smoke. She didn't care who heard her. She strutted through the main artery of Sebastian High School, unaware of who noticed her and who didn't.

She liked the way her Manolos clicked in stylized rhythm along the lacquered tile, and she liked even better how the skirt she wore, black and short, kept sliding up and up, exposing more and more leg. She knew the boys were looking at her, trying to see as far north as they could. But she wasn't wearing this for them. In the trophy case, in that shimmering shelf of all things varsity and suburban, she looked beyond the Sebastian High School yearbook snapshots of bygone victories and gold-plated testimonies to races won and hurdles cleared. In the reflection of the recently polished glass, she looked only at herself. Stunning was the obvious word. Raven's hair, a river of it, lined her almond face, the emerald eyes. Her hand slid down the outline of her body. Perfect.

"Knock, knock," she said as she entered. And there he was. Mr. Natolly. "Bill," she said.

He turned from the white board.

"Tamara," he said. He looked good. He always looked good; whether he was explaining the double entendre of a Byron sonnet, or cleaning the dry erase board. He had just enough geek, just enough humor, endless intelligence, and a great ass. He rubbed his fingers absentmindedly through his thick head of hair and adopted an Oxford smile, a smile that found only one side of his mouth, like a crooked anchor. He put down his pen and walked towards her. As he neared her, he intensified his gaze. He smelled her neck, then moved past her. He went to the door and locked it with a firm twist. He went back to her.

"Tamara," he said again, and this time he sounded like a little boy. A little boy who needed something. His hand found the hem of her dress. He fingered the fabric, rubbing it back and forth. He let the fabric go and his fingers found her face. He brushed her cheek. She blanched.

"Mr. Natolly," she said. He looked deep in her eyes. "Do you like this?" He asked, his voice back to being a man.

"Like what?" she asked.

He stuck his hand straight up Tamara's black skirt. His other hand was inside her blouse. She had no choice but to let a moan escape.

"I guess that's a yes," Bill said.

"This is my first time."

"I know. It won't hurt. Well, it might a little. But only for a few seconds."

He slipped off her panties and threw them down on the floor. He lifted her on top of a desk. She tried her best to remember who sat there in homeroom. Some Jane or John. He pushed her knees up and unbuckled his belt. His pants fell to the floor.

He bent her over the desk. She could feel the hair on his arms race up and down her back as he pushed into her.

"Perfect," was all he said.

"Perfect," was all she said back.

And then she realized they weren't alone. She could hear snickers. Old boring snickers of teens who didn't yet know how to be adults.

She found herself staring at the window, her teacher pounding into her. And she wasn't the girl who was reflected in the glass of the trophy case. She was ugly. Beyond ugly. Her dark hair, that raven's nest of blackness, turned gray and brittle and frayed.

Her polished skin went from lacquered to pale, alabaster to wrinkled, her green eyes found cataracts and dullness.

And then he, her first, realized how she'd changed. He stopped fucking her.

"No," she said. "Don't stop," she urged.

Mr. Natolly was looking at her like a foreign object. Tamara closed her eyes.

"Please don't stop."

He pulled out of her.

"No," she pleaded.

The snickers around her built to a crescendo of vicious laughter. The kids, those feckless masses of students, began to chant her name like a pep rally gone sour.

"TAMARA, TAMARA, TAMARA!"

Mr. Natolly buttoned up his corduroys and walked back to the dry erase board.

"Mr. Natolly, please come back. You love me," she said in a soporific whisper.

He turned. Scoffed.

"No one can love you."

"No," Tamara said. And then she repeated it. Over and over. "No. No. No!"

And then she was in a new nightmare. But this one was real. She was in the middle of English class, muttering the word "no" like some idiot savant. The teacher she'd just envisioned fucking her had stopped his lecture. On the dry erase board was the title: DUALITY OF MAN.

"Tamara?"

She didn't want to look at Mr. Natolly, afraid that he might somehow have the power to read her thoughts. See her hidden desire. She faked a smile and then looked at her reflection in the window. She wasn't the hag she'd become in her daydream, but she wasn't gorgeous, either. She was marred by acne scars and thin hair, by a too round face and gypsy eyes. She quit looking at herself and focused beyond her plainness, gazing upon the large, crooked elm tree with the twisted roots and deep green foliage that hung like a canopy over the freshman quad outside.

"Sorry," she said quietly, still looking at the tree.

"You okay?"

She nodded. But the nod was a lie, as they often were.

"Good. So, as I was saying, a common theme in literature is duality. It's in every book we read. The Bible had Cain and Abel. Shakespeare had Iago and Ophelia. Pop culture has Lady Gaga."

"She's over," said Patrick, a 19-year-old slacker with a John Hughes bad boy veneer. He was attempting to graduate for the second consecutive year.

"Not the point," Mr. Natolly said. "The point is we're all waiting for her to choose a side. Be it dark or light. And interesting characters must choose. It's why we read books and watch TV and listen to music. They argue, either with another character, or themselves, or God or whatever, trying desperately to make the right choice."

Tamara was barely listening to the lecture. She felt dirty after her daydream. But then she remembered she had something, maybe the only thing, that gave her a sense of calm, in the eye of any storm. Tamara had a secret. It wasn't just her daydream about her English teacher or her fear of reflections. It was something hidden in her book bag. She knew she should leave it there, closed and gathering dust. She knew it was something she shouldn't bother with. But, she kept imagining that girl in her fantasy, the one who sauntered down the school hallway without any cares at all. She pried her eyes off the elm tree and reached for the backpack that hung off her chair. She unzipped it and pulled a book out.

"So, was it the devil that made Cain kill his brother? Or caused Iago to cause so much havoc? Was it something evil that coerced Ophelia into drowning? Or made Gaga try too hard? Or was it something inherent within them? Was John Wayne Gacy a monster, or just really sick? What are the key moments in anyone's life, be it a character in a novel, or a friend, when a good person turns bad or a good person stays good?" Mr. Natolly asked the class. The faces of the students expressed many versions of the same feeling: boredom.

Tamara let her fingers trace the embossed title of the book. Behind her, Patrick was planning an attack and rifled a spitball at her. Tamara yelped, jumped up and dropped her book. The class laughed at Tamara, this time for real.

"Book of Shadows: A Modern Woman's Journey Into Witchcraft," Patrick read out loud, after picking up the book that had fallen. "It looks like you've already made that journey, Tam, and by the looks of it, I'd say it was one helluva rough trip."

Two other students, Chloe and Jesse, who both had desks next to Tamara, gave each other exasperated looks. Patrick was one of those class clowns who only thought he was the life of the party. Next to Patrick, Shawn, a muscled jock and Patrick's partner in crime gave him a quick high five.

"Patrick, enough. I don't want to be teaching you for a third year. So just shut it," Mr. Natolly said with fervor. "What anyone chooses to read is up to them. I personally commend Tamara for stepping outside the box and trying to glean knowledge on unusual topics. And, speaking of reading, I want you all to grab the new Gazette. It has an interesting essay entitled "Steroids on Main Street." It was written by our Tamara and it's a riveting article."

The bell rang and the kids got up, grabbed the requisite Gazette and shuffled out of the door and into the next class. Tamara remained.

"Mr. Natolly," Tamara said.

"Sorry about Patrick. He's nearly my age. Boy is just trouble."

"Those were my personal thoughts," she said as she twisted her hair nervously with her finger.

"And your thoughts were wonderful. The Board asked me to pick the best of the best and, of course, I picked you. You're my star pupil. If this was the NBA, you'd be Lebron," he said, folding his arms over his chest.

For a moment she felt just as beautiful as she did in her daydream, before it turned bad.

"I just wanted the article to be for you," she said.

"With a mind like yours, we need to share your gifts," Mr. Natolly said. Then he took out a handkerchief from his front pocket and wiped his brow. "I don't know why they're afraid to turn on the air conditioning in this place."

"But the article. What if people get hurt by it? That wasn't what I wanted," she said. "The last thing I want to do is get someone in trouble."

"You'll incite change," he said. He put his handkerchief down on a desk and focused all his attention on Tamara. "It's the curse of the self-possessed, Tamara."

"Are you sure?" Tamara asked. She quit twisting her hair.

"Of course I'm sure. You did good, kid. You should be proud," he said. Tamara beamed in the glow of his praise. She even allowed herself a real smile. Then, the door opened.

"I heard someone gave a riveting lecture on Wuthering Heights, or Jane Eyre or some old book that no one reads anymore," an attractive woman said, her hair up in a studious bun.

"Allison," Mr. Natolly said to the woman. "I don't need any 'guidance'."

"You don't need guidance and I'm the guidance counselor. Good play on words," She said, then kissed her husband hard on the lips and pulled away, playfully grabbing his face. "You realize you use that line at least twice a week?" She smiled and kissed him again.

Bill unlocked his lips and looked for Tamara. She was gone.

"Weird. Tamara was just here. I told her about her article being published."

"Well, now it's just us," Allison said, her lean good looks too much for Bill to resist. They kissed again. And then again.

Chapter 2

Stickers. Adhesives. Tamara had a menagerie of them on her locker. They were often dated: LOSER, I'M WITH STUPID, FAT CHICKS DO IT HOT-N-HEAVY, but each one stung a bit, despite the fact she knew they shouldn't. Knowing and feeling were mutually exclusive notions for Tamara.

She slid over her algebra book and held onto a Cat's Eye shell. It was something she'd found online at www.thewitchesbrew.com. The book about witches wasn't just a plaything. The book, the daydreams, and the sadness were more than just hobbies. They gave Tamara a sense of calm in the chaos.

"Bitch," Shawn said, sticking a "My Name Is Moron" sticker on the back of Tamara's crimson locker. Shawn was Ken doll handsome. Blonde, blue-eyed and bland, he possessed qualities that most people in his world found unyieldingly attractive.

"I'm sorry?" Tamara asked, not used to being directly talked to. She was comfortable in the shadows, or being the punch line of a joke, even if it was a sad comfort.

"Why'd you write this stupid article?" Shawn said, the irritation obvious by his furrowed brow.

"I'm...I..." Tamara stumbled for words. An apology. But they eluded her.

"Oh, now you've got nothing to say? You should have had that problem earlier."

He showed Tamara the Gazette, with her article on steroid use in high school sports. Shawn, the star athlete in three different sports, was the obvious "user."

"I just meant for Mr. Natolly to read that. They were my private thoughts." Tamara said.

Shawn ignored her, like everyone. He read from the article verbatim in a mocking tone, high pitched and too animated.

"It's no secret that some of our star athletes are taking performance enhancing drugs. But the coaches ignore them because they care more about the State Championships than they do about the players."

Patrick, in all his white trash glory, came up behind Shawn and grabbed the newspaper.

"Busted. I knew your guns were fake," Patrick said, squeezing Shawn's bicep.

"Shut up, dick," Shawn said, and threatened him with a punch flinch move. Shawn turned back to Tamara. "Because of you I have to piss in a cup." He took the Gazette back from Patrick and stormed down the hall.

Patrick eyed Tamara's Cat's Eye shell. And, copying Shawn, punch-flinched her. She dropped the charm on the floor. Patrick, wasting no time, stepped on it and crushed it. Tamara looked at the jagged pieces and her face went slack. Patrick, proud of himself, took a step back and bumped into Roger, a classic geek born with a cleft chin and a brain the size of a small state. Patrick hated him for all the reasons stated above.

"Watch it, techno nerd," Patrick spewed, the residue of the Cat's Eye shell still on his sneakers.

"Two years as the resident senior idiot, and that's all you can come up with?" Roger asked. He carried a stack of wires piled on an archaic VCR.

"Fag," Patrick said, his monosyllabic stab at redemption.

"Much better. Consider me insulted. Really," Roger said with no conviction, and walked away.

Patrick realized he was trumped. He turned to Tamara to hurl some new insult, but she was gone. Her locker closed.

Chapter 3

Tamara sat on the edge of a bench in the gym locker room. She looked around the large, open space. More lockers, more girls whispering things to other girls, the smell of wet towels. But what she was really looking for was more trauma hurled her way. Bad things happened to girls like her in places like a gym locker room. She knew it, and a part of her was just waiting for it to happen, whatever "it" was. And there was always an "it."

Kisha, the queen bee of the school, a gracefully stunning African American senior with disarming flecks of gold in her mocha-colored eyes, came into the locker room with her cabal of cheerleaders close behind her. They were like geese flying in formations, heading south. Due Tamara.

"Oh shit," Kisha said. "Somebody call animal control. One of their drug-sniffing dogs is off its leash."

The girls laughed. Kisha, to add insult to injury, threw her sweaty towel at Tamara, who sat there, stuck in her learned helplessness of accepting her fate as a punching bag.

"Fuck off, Kisha. Take that towel and shove it up your ass."

Tamara, and everyone, turned to see who had said that. Who dared tempt the lioness? It was Chloe. She had short, spiky hair. She looked punk rock in an age of pop tarts. She was wearing only panties and she looked hard and tough, despite the kitten print on her underwear. She threw the towel back at Kisha.

"Courtney Love died a long time ago. Bitch," Kisha said. She threw the towel back at Chloe. "Mind your own business."

"Mind my own business? Lame. Pick on someone your own size."

One of Kisha's girls stepped up into Chloe's face. Their noses nearly touched, but Chloe didn't pull away.

"Screw these two losers. We don't have time to throw down with Morticia and the Hag."

The girl backed down and Kisha and her crew left the locker room.

"You okay?" Chloe said to Tamara. Tamara nodded. "Those girls are so tired. They're hot shit now. But in ten years, they'll all be fat, alcoholic, single mothers. Mark my words. Oprah and Stephen King were us in high school. We are the game changers."

Tamara smiled and gently tossed the towel that Kisha had thrown at Chloe into a large laundry bin.

"Is that a smile?" Chloe asked as she grabbed a clean towel.

"I guess it is," Tamara said.

*

Tamara loved the hot water of the shower. It rained over her like some liquid cure curing an unknown disease. She let her dark hair get drenched. Across the stall from her, Tamara could see in to Chloe's stall. The shower curtain was open. Just enough. Chloe had just finished rinsing her hair. Tamara took a glance. She really was a throwback to the Riot Grrls of yesteryear. Rail thin, most likely blessed with a good metabolism and a low hunger drive. She wasn't really remarkable save for that pixie cut of hair.

Tamara turned off her shower. So did Chloe. Tamara opened her shower curtain just a bit. And she saw Chloe do the same. Tamara felt the water drip down from her face onto her slight paunch of a stomach. And then Chloe looked at the stall next to Tamara's. Some unknown girl, marginally attractive and no doubt one of Kisha's fan club members, showered. Chloe's eyes were focused on the girl; they resembled Tamara's unfettered gaze when she looked at Mr. Natolly. Wide-eyed. Open.

"Chloe?" Tamara said.

"What the fuck?" Chloe said to Tamara, quickly readjusting her sight line away from the girl. "I was just rinsing off."

"It's okay," Tamara said.

"Freak," Chloe said, way too quickly. She grabbed her towel, wrapped it around her body, didn't look back at either Tamara or Kisha's friend, and went into the locker room.

Alliances build and melt away like butter on bread. Easily.

*

Showered and clean, Tamara was dressed and ready to make the best of the rest of the day. She set off down the labyrinth of long hallways that connected the many classrooms of her high school. Sure, the day started off bad, but it ended somewhat decent, which was a victory to her. Except for the strange exchange with Chloe in the shower. But that moment didn't matter in the big scheme of things. Tamara chose to focus on the small battles won in showers and lockers and towels tossed at the wrong girl. It made the school seem less scary, for once. She didn't miss her Cat Eye's shell charm, or her daydream with Mr. Natolly. Sometimes reality wasn't so bad, she told herself. She felt herself strut, just a bit. Her arms relaxed by her side. Then, from down the hallway, she saw a dust storm of activity, heard the echoes of guttural yells and shouts. Tamara slumped back into herself and her fists clenched into little balls of tension. Reality had turned back to its normal form of nervous, acute fear.

The boys, the crew, the pack, whatever it is they called themselves, were nearing Tamara. It was the usual suspects. Shawn and Patrick and a few others whose names she couldn't remember. She clutched the straps on her backpack, like a skydiver ready to release the chute. She panicked and thought she should just enter a classroom, any classroom, to avoid them.

She tried a door, but it was locked.

The guys were now twenty feet away from her. She had no choice but to try her best to turn invisible. She walked slowly west and they walked quickly east. She tried to evaporate into a locker. Her anxiety swelled like a Pacific wave. Think of Chloe, she told herself, as if Chloe's earlier kindness could act like some sort of shield against the shrapnel that was about to be hurled her way.

The boys were now upon her.

The witch's book, she told herself, when Chloe's kindness proved to be futile at abating her anxiety. Witches never succumbed to anything, she told herself. They didn't have to. They had the power of magic to protect them. She took a few deep breaths. And she saw herself, once again, standing near the same trophy case she had stood in front of in her daydream. She looked past the erstwhile, gold-plated success of students past. She closed her eyes, waiting for the barrage of the boys.

To her pleasant surprise, and relative shock, Shawn, Patrick and their friends, ignored her. Her attempt at invisibility somehow succeeded. Before she had a chance to celebrate this tiny victory, she realized the reason the boys bypassed her. Mr. Natolly stood in his office door. He called to her.

"Glad I found you. I feel like a jerk," he said, as he led her into the room. "I should have never published that article."

"It's fine." But it wasn't fine. Tamara was trying her best to convince both herself and Mr. Natolly that what he had done wasn't a big deal. "You liked my article. So, it's fine."

"My mother said that right before she killed herself," Mr. Natolly said wryly.

Tamara's jaw dropped. She tried to say something, but no words came to her.

"God, what a horrible joke," he said, shaking his head. "I forget you're 17. Even if you were 35, that would be a bad joke."

"Did your mother really do that?" Tamara asked nervously.

"Has anyone bothered you? About the article?" He asked, ignoring her question and erasing, "Duality of Man" from the board.

Tamara just stood there. Silent.

Mr. Natolly smiled. Then he spoke in a sweet whisper. "Yes, my mother really chose that ending for herself. She had her reasons. And sometimes I use humor, macabre humor, to help remind myself how funny life can be."

"Like Ignatius in A Confederacy of Dunces?" Tamara asked.

"Exactly! Literature, art, it reminds us that, no matter how bad things are in life, no matter how hard it is for us to understand the actions of others, we have a universal longing to feel connected."

"To feel like we belong," Tamara added.

"Exactly! That mind of yours, Tamara," he said.

Outside, peals of laughter, and then a faint scream filled the classroom.

Tamara flinched at the sound.

"No doubt Patrick torturing some poor freshman," Mr. Natolly said. He then walked up to Tamara and put his hands on her shoulders. "I'm sorry. I shouldn't have published that article. I thought I was helping you out."

"Shawn already laid into me."

"Again, I'm so sorry, Tamara."

"I know. It's just. I told you that was just for you."

"You know, the writer of Confederacy of Dunces committed suicide without anyone reading his book. His mother found it, long after he died, and got it out there."

"I'm not going to do that," Tamara said.

Mr. Natolly let his hands drop from her shoulders. "I know. Listen, doesn't it say in the Bible that this too shall pass? In a few years, no one will care."

"Chloe said the same thing."

"Chloe?"

"Some chick," Tamara said.

"A friend?"

"No. Just a girl who didn't throw towels." Tamara blanched a bit at this.

"One of my favorite writers, a Portuguese poet, Fernando Pessoa, once said that literature is the easiest way to ignore life."

"I'm not reading a book, Mr. Natolly. I would love to ignore life." She thought about her book on witchcraft. She thought about it over and over.

"Call me Bill."

"Bill."

"Ignoring life is the cheap way out, Tamara. Life is meant for the breathing and living. Come on, let's go," Bill said. The two left the classroom and walked into the hallway.

"Tyger, Tyger, burning bright," she said to him, desperate for the moment between the two of them to last just a little longer. "What immortal hands could frame thy perfect symmetry," she continued.

Then Bill took over. "In what distant deeps or skies, burnt the fire of thine eyes? On what wings dare he aspire? What the hand dare seize the fire?"

Completely enraptured, she reached over and did something impetuous and riotous. She kissed his hand. She dared seize it, like Byron had asked those who were willing to do. This wasn't a bad dream or a good dream. This wasn't a poem. This was real life. She kissed his hand, which had just the right amount of hair on it, just the right amount of smoothness and callousness. And just the right amount of something she never should have done.

"I'm sorry."

"I'm sorry."

It didn't matter who said it first or second. They both knew it was wrong. And even worse, Kisha had just sauntered down the hallway, humming the new Miley Cyrus song. She saw the kiss and ducked behind a locker. Listening.

Tamara stared at Mr. Natolly. Humiliated, "I'm so stupid."

"No, you're not. And you're going to find someone. Someone who loves you for all of your gifts and maybe even a few of your flaws," Mr. Natolly said.

"Holy shit," Kisha said quietly and then grinned a Cheshire grin. "Holy shit."

Chapter 4

That night, Patrick stood outside a car in this small town's version of Lover's Lane. It was actually just a dirt parking lot near a man-made lake, now waterless, that was originally supposed to be a new housing project for upper class rich men. But none of that worked out. What remained was the skeleton of thwarted progress, taken over by kids trying to fuck their way into adulthood. The lake bed remained a gutted and dusty failure. A few other cars were parked there, rippling with teenage sex.

In the car, Shawn's father's Corvette, he and Kisha groped and teased. The Ken doll and the cheerleader.

"Babe, you've put on some weight," Shawn said as he leaned into her. She pushed him away.

"Really? Now's when you decide to play that card?"

"I'm not saying it's a bad thing."

"Just because I'm not some scrawny white ass starving bitch?"

"Kisha."

"Shawn."

He leaned in to kiss her again, and she pulled away again.

"Mood's over. And so is your chance. Plus, we have that idiot Patrick watching us."

They both got out of the car, Shawn trying to hide his untamed excitement in the presence of Patrick.

"You two done playing doctor?" Patrick said.

"Before it even started," Kisha said.

"Good. 'Cause I have what you asked for," Patrick said and showed Shawn a little baggie of pills that he pulled from his pocket.

The late afternoon had turned to dusk and the air had a hum of coolness. Kisha reached back in the car for her hoodie.

"I heard, dude," Patrick said to Shawn.

"Heard what?" Kisha asked as she put on her jacket.

"I don't want to talk it about it," Shawn said.

But Patrick did. He turned to Kisha, "That freak got your future Pro Bowl quarterback hubby suspended." Patrick held up his pills. "She ruined my job and his career."

Kisha looked at Shawn. His face told the truth.

"So that's why," she said, referring to what occurred in the Corvette.

"Why what?" Patrick asked.

"Nothing. Yeah, coach benched me. I might not be eligible for All-State," Shawn said, and he said it with a little boy's voice. Kisha moved over and put her arms around him.

"It's okay, babe."

"It's not okay," Shawn said. "This is my future. Our future."

"It's Tamara's fault," Patrick said. "Her life sucks, so she's gotta bring the rest of us down. We need to get that bitch."

Kisha tugged on the sleeves of her sweater. "Well, I know something."

Shawn pulled her close. "I'm sorry, babe. About what I said." They kissed. "Now spill."

"Tamara made a move on Natolly and he shot her down. It was so sad and embarrassing. He said something like, 'you'll find someone who loves you for your gifts and flaws, or whatever." Kisha felt the thin layer of fat on her belly and then let it go. "As if that ever happens."

"He's married," said Shawn.

"And she's disgusting. I swear, every time I see her, my dick crawls up inside my body," Patrick said with a shudder.

Shawn looked at the moon, just as a cloud obscured it.

"I think Tamara needs to be taught a lesson. She screwed up my life," Shawn said.

"Mine too." Patrick added. He put the baggie of pills in his pocket. "I can't sell my shit now and college ain't gonna pay for itself."

Shawn rolled his eyes. "Yeah, I don't think money's your problem there."

He turned to Kisha. "She has a thing for Natolly?" he said as an evil grin wrapped around his face. "Well, that's easy enough."

*

Allison Natolly thumbed through a new book on Jung as she sat on her couch. The living room was an extension of her. Warm. Comfortable. Earthy. Outside the window, the light from the sickle-cell shaped moon beamed in like a beacon. She heard the door open. She put down the book.

"Jung?" Bill said.

"I'm into dreams these days. I actually don't believe a word of it, but wouldn't it be nice if dreams did mean something?"

Bill leaned in to kiss her. She felt his face and pulled him closer. He pulled away.

"What's wrong?" she asked.

"Just an odd day. Think it calls for three fingers of Scotch."

"On a Tuesday?"

"A really odd day, hon." He wiped his brow and walked into the kitchen. He poured his drink. Then searched the fridge for some comfort food.

Allison reached for a bowl and heated up some corn chowder. She knew his favorite. "Care to share?"

"Tamara."

"Yes? Brightest student in your class."

"She has a crush on me."

Allison laughed. "Of course she does. Every girl does."

"She actually tried to kiss me."

The microwave beeped its readiness. Allison opened it, and then dug in a drawer for a spoon. "Sit down. Drink your Scotch. Eat your soup."

Bill did as he was told. Allison sat next to him and watched his every spoonful. And his every small nip of the amber drink.

"What?" he asked.

"This wasn't a bad day. I think in some ways Tamara thinks of you as a dad. A caretaker."

"Is that supposed to make me feel good? Or creepy?" He slurped a spoonful of soup.

"I hope it's a girl," Allison said.

Bill took another spoonful of the soup. Then a sip of the amber. Both warmed his body in a perfect way. Then he saw the moon outside. That perfect upside down sickle. He made eye contact with Allison. Saw tears of joy in her eyes. He knew why.

"Are you sure?" he asked tentatively.

She nodded. He leaned in and kissed her.

"It happened. Finally." Allison said.

Bill pushed the soup and his drink away and lifted Allison up on the table. "We're gonna have a baby. Our baby, Bill. Your baby."

"I want to make five more tonight," he said.

Chapter 5

The day stayed cool and crisp. A good Midwestern fall day, the leaves had turned their colors and the snow remained aloof.

Shawn had found his Homecoming King charm. He walked around the school chatting with people outside of his circle, with anyone who'd listen to him. It was almost as if he was trying to make up for the article by harnessing goodwill from the unwashed masses of those not normally deemed cool. This, of course, couldn't be further from the truth. Shawn wasn't slumming it without a purpose. He was looking for one person in particular.

"Roger!" Shawn yelled across the grassy quad. Roger looked over at him and shrugged. Shawn called out to him.

"Having a huge party tonight. I want you there, man," Shawn said, as he approached Roger, slapping him playfully on the shoulder.

"Um. You're Andrew Luck. I'm Steve Jobs. We don't party together."

"Senior year. I'm changing all that nonsense. These are the best times of our lives. We need to all come together," Shawn said.

"But you haven't spoken to me in, like, decades," Roger rebutted.

"Roger, we were neighbors, we grew up together, I went to your first and second grade birthday parties. I feel bad we've drifted."

Roger just stood there, unable to respond.

"Just come. The party will be the party to end all parties. Oh and tell your mother hello. She still have that crazy perm? I used to love those sugar cookies she made."

Behind Roger, Chloe and her friend, Jesse, walked up.

"Did you say party to end all parties?" Jesse asked.

Chloe punched Jesse in the back, as if to warn him that he was speaking to someone he shouldn't be. She hated Shawn, but was reticent to say it. Jesse, in his new wave retro punk rock attire, hated nothing but bad music and his new life far away from his beloved place of birth, Los Angeles.

"Just moved here. Chloe's the only cool chick I've found." Jesse said, extending his fist for a bump.

"Do I know you?" Shawn asked, without touching Jesse's fist.

"Nope. Just moved from Silverlake. Part of LA. I know you, though. Leader of men here in Small Town, USA. I'm down with that. In LA on every night of the week, I could find some rave. So I hear party? I get excited. I like your hair."

Shawn's hair was a simple fade. Jesse had a Mohawk and blonde tips.

Roger watched all of this with a child's fascination. Cool kids, of two varieties, punk and jock, having a meeting of the minds, and he was at the epicenter. He had in his hands two DVDs of Doctor Who, and he quietly placed them in his pocket.

Shawn eyed Jesse. "You think you can maybe get some weed?"

"Weed?" Jesse asked, with a mocking laugh. "Nah."

"You bring the party, then you can come to the party," Shawn said with a smile.

Chloe turned to Jesse as if she could will him to turn down Shawn's offer. But it didn't work.

"Awesome." Jesse said. "We're coming. But we play my choice of music. I was in a band."

"Sounds great," Shawn said.

Chloe sighed. She and Jesse left. Roger and Shawn stood in the quad. There was an awkward moment as they both looked around at the haves and have nots that circled them. Finally Shawn broke the silence.

"Will you be there?" Shawn asked.

"Yeah. Yeah. I'll be there."

"Good," Shawn said.

Roger started to follow Chloe and Jesse back towards class.

"Roger?" Shawn yelled.

"Yeah?" Roger asked, looking over his shoulder.

"You're still part of the A/V Club, right?"

Chapter 6

After school, after another day of avoiding Shawn and Patrick and Kisha, and sitting in a bathroom stall during most of English class, Tamara heard the final bell. She hurried towards the double doors that led to freedom from those hallowed halls. She saw Chloe and Jesse up ahead and mustered a wave. They gave two back. Then Tamara pushed through the door and went home.

Home was an inaccurate word for where Tamara lived. It was like saying peace in Iran. Home was a repair shop on Crossmore Avenue. Not just the wrong the side of the tracks, but the side of town that had no tracks. No way in and no way out. She opened the front door. The bell over the door heralded her entrance. She heard a moan from inside the living room. She walked past the carcasses of dead radios and TVs and fax machines and other items that desperately needed attention, but would never receive it. A repair shop where nothing was ever fixed seemed to be the perfect embodiment of her life.

"Tam?" her father bellowed.

"Home, Dad," she called to him. She thought maybe she should go and check up on him.

"'Bout time."

"School just ended."

"Don't think I know that?"

He'd already started drinking. She could tell by his subtle slurring. She thought better about checking up on him. She went to the creaking staircase and ascended it. She escaped the pallor and grime of the downstairs technological graveyard, his world, and entered her own.

Tamara's little room overlooking Crossmore was the one place she truly felt safe. She barely decorated it. Just simple, Spartan living, with a desk, a dresser, a small bed with a bedspread that had a tiger embroidered in felt. Next to the bed was a stack of newspapers with dozens of crossword puzzles that she'd finished, all in black ink. It wasn't much, but it was all hers.

She sat on her bed and retrieved the crushed Cat Eye's shell from her bag. She put it back together as best she could. Then she took out Book of Shadows: A Modern Woman's Journey Into Witchcraft from her backpack and thumbed through the pages.

Suddenly, her door flung open.

"What the hell you doing? The storage room needs cleaning." Her father was wearing a stained T-shirt and jeans that snugged too tight. He had a beer in hand. His hair was full and black and one got the sense that if things had turned out a little different, if more people needed things fixed, or if he had the wherewithal to actually do cogent work, he might have ended up a better man. Or if she, Tamara's mother, had just lived.

"Dad, I've had a tough day and lots of homework."

He took his umpteenth swill of beer.

"And my day's been better?"

"I don't want to fight."

She tried to hide her book and the shell. He saw it and stormed towards her.

"You stole that from her? The one thing I hated? You can't cook. Won't clean. But you find time to play witch games with her stupid books? She died of cancer and no amount of witchcraft saved her. And no amount will save you," he said, as Tamara stood silent.

He shut the door, tripping over an unseen barrier and passed out in the middle of the hallway, right between a picture of Eisenhower that had fallen off the wall, and a portable radio he'd wanted to build with the son he never had.

Later, Tamara, with the book firmly in her grip, stepped over him, after she heard his breathing grow deep and rhythmic.

She went into the only other room on the second floor. Her mother's room. The room was caught in a time warp. Everything remained exactly how it was the day her mother died. It had the faint odor of her mother, a patchwork scent of patchouli, lavender, and rain. On a small table in the corner, the sewing machine that Tamara had sewn her Halloween costume with, when she went as the Cowardly Lion in sixth grade, remained threaded. A collection of strawberry figurines gathered dust in their respective homes on shelves and the windowpane. And, of course, her mother's fabled collection of Bibles. Tamara didn't care for them, but her mother had found comfort in them.

But Tamara's focus went to the giant bookshelf that lined the entirety of one wall. Filled with books of all genres. Tamara admired the countless tomes as she slid the book she held onto the shelf. Mr. Natolly would love this room, she thought. As she made a mental inventory of the books, Tamara found herself drawn to one particular shelf filled with books on magic. She pulled out a few books about spells, solstices, paganism.

As she flipped through the pages, her mind wandered. She thought of school and her classmates. Even though Tamara wished she were a part of the world that included the focused Shawn, the irreverent Patrick, the perfect Kisha and the hipster chic of Chloe and Jesse, she knew she was too odd, reserved, awkward and ugly to ever orbit in their universe.

But Mr. Natolly. He got her. And even though Allison was a nice enough woman, she wasn't his woman. Or she should not have been. It should be me, Tamara thought. She said it to herself again, even as she heard her father stir in the hallway. Something in her told her it was time to not just peruse her mother's library, but to actually study the words on the pages. She stopped flipping through the books, sat with folded legs, and began to read, slowly, savoring the words. These words weren't able to help her mother's liver cancer, but maybe they'd be able to help Tamara's social cancer. And, she thought with a smile, Mr. Natolly did tell her she was his star pupil. Studying seemed to be her only real talent.

She found a book called Love Works in Ten Words, written by some Druid ancient. She found one called Babies For Prophets, written by a Muslim mystic in the days following Mohammed's death. They were interesting reads, but she wasn't drawn to either of them. She kept looking.

Eventually, she found a small, worn book, which was tagged repeatedly with her mother's handwriting. Her squiggles and underlines and earmarks made Tamara think she must have inherited her mother's studious nature. The name of the book was True Love Doesn't Die. Tamara never bothered to look at the author's name.

The parchment was very old and fragile. Tamara wondered if this was the last book her mother read. She thought maybe it was. Maybe the book, this one book was a portent of good things to come. She held it to her chest like a living sacrament. As if it were her mom. Then she opened it. She gently turned the pages.

Chapter titles included: "Sons & Daughters," "Flora & Fauna," "Husbands & Wives," "Ghosts & Dreams," and, finally, "Requited & Unrequited." Each chapter had specific spells that would ensure true love for each given entity. Tamara's Catholic school upbringing made her a bit hesitant, but her mother's death, and her comforting handwriting on the brittle pages, combined with her own desperation, allowed her to not give a damn. It was now or never.

Tamara grabbed some cloth from the sewing machine on the table in the corner. Then she picked up a strawberry figurine made to look human by black paint strategically positioned to resemble a smiling person, some silly plastic Eiffel Tower from her mother's final dream trip to France, and a King James Bible that had pages lined with gold leafing. She spread these objects out over a baby-changing table that she'd found hidden in the closet.

She took out Mr. Natolly's handkerchief, the one she stole when Allison had entered the classroom that morning, took a deep breath, and then began to recite a spell.

"Ama me," she said in Latin, as the book instructed her.

"Ama me. Ama me." She clutched the handkerchief tightly.

"What the hell you doing in here?" Her dad had woken up. Another beer was in his right hand.

"Nothing," she said weakly.

"I told you I needed something to eat."

He saw her mother's books.

"You're not Carrie. This isn't a Stephen King novel. You're mother's dead and you're never going to be prom queen." His eyes were glossy and red. He stared at her for a few moments, and then shut the door. Tamara clutched the handkerchief.

"Ama me," she said. "Love me." Tamara heard her father trip and fall. She went out to the hall to make sure he was still breathing. He was. Tamara went back into the room. She inhaled.

"To the ancients who were here before time, hear my prayers. I supplicate myself to you, asking for your favor. I say these words from the ever-hungry belly of despair, from a place of no return, from the hope in all things true and sacred. From eternal love. "

*

Across town, Allison returned home from the store. She put her bag packed with healthy food on the counter. Then removed Bill's corn chowder and a bottle of anti-nausea medicine for herself. She knew what was coming, the morning sickness, and she couldn't wait for it. She hoped the pink of the bottle was a silly portent for a baby girl. The pains of motherhood weren't going to be pleasant, but what a small price to pay for the miracle that grew inside of her. She reached for her keys. They fumbled in her grasp and fell behind the counter.

Tamara, still in her mother's room, wished for the things that her mother had wished for. She wished her father wasn't a drunk. She wished for love. Wished for a bigger life. She carried on, steadfast and focused, the way her father would with his beer.

"To the old ones, endowed with powers of love and attraction, bind my fate to that of the one I desire.

*

Across town, far from Crossmore, Allison found her keys on a pile of cobwebs. She sighed. The maid needed to do a more thorough job. Allison pinned the keys on the hook and called out to Bill, who she knew was watching the game in the bedroom upstairs.

"Bill?" she yelled. "Got more of your soup."

*

Tamara lit one of her mother's many candles. She watched the smoke drift up towards the ceiling. The flame was weak, but it was still fire. She let the heat pass over her fingers.
"My mother knew this pain. It means nothing. It's just momentary," she told herself. Then she blew out the candle.

*

Allison called out to Bill again. He didn't respond. She went upstairs to find him lying on the bed, the TV humming gently, a glass of Scotch, empty, on the bedside table. And next to the glass, was the bottle. Nearly emptied. Bill's breath made his stomach balloon in and out. Allison sat next to him. She looked at him and ran her fingers through his hair. She put her hand on his heaving stomach. Then she put her other hand on her own stomach. It made her smile in that safe way you do when you know you're loved. She put the chowder on the table, next to the empty glass.

*

"Like this flame, my mother's flame. Let me rise like a Phoenix and reclaim all that is mine. Not just mine. But my mother's too." Tamara relit the candle and the flame came back like an arsonist's dream. It was five times as strong as the first flame.

*

"Bill? Honey?" Allison said. She wanted to talk. Bill shifted. He lifted his head, still mostly asleep, and said something that Allison couldn't comprehend. She laughed.

"Did you just say Boo Radley?"

He didn't respond. He put his head on her lap and fell back asleep. She kissed his forehead and saw the moon from the large, bay window.

"Luna. That's going to be her name. Luna," she said.

Bill muffled the same word in a drowned out tone.

Knowing he was fine, Allison gently lifted his head and slid off the bed. She walked downstairs.

*

In Tamara's mother's room, the candle went out. The room was dark, save for the white luminescence of the sickle cell moon that shone in from the bedroom.

"With a touch, grant me the power to sway others to do my bidding."

The candle burned bright again.

*

Allison had put away the groceries and now felt the crush of sleep weighing on her. She turned off the lights and climbed the stairs. She began to walk down the hall to her bedroom. The house seemed too quiet and Allison felt that twinge of panic she sometimes felt when she was alone, in the dark. The silence gave her pause. An eerie, deathly silence made her hold onto her belly, to Luna.

Suddenly, from downstairs, Allison heard a loud crash. It made no sense, in the middle of the night. She screamed, then started to rush to Bill, to their bedroom. But a figure emerged from the shadows. Stopping her in her tracks.

"Who's there?" she said, her breath quickening. The figure was now upon her. It seemed to be placing its hand on her chest, holding her in a state of paralysis.

"It's a dream," she told herself. Her mother used to sing her hymns when things would go bump in the night and she thought that's all this was. She sang to herself, "Swing Low," in a flat, quivering tone. She just wanted to get down the hall. But she couldn't move.

"Cunt."

The word rang out like a banshee on the moor. Allison was positive she had heard it. The hand on her chest softened and Allison didn't hesitate with her newly found freedom. She ran down the stairs. She passed the den, passed the drink Bill had left on the table. Again, she held her belly.

She rubbed her leg. She had a scar there. Lizard long. Allison started to move, but halted when she sensed something behind her. She slowly turned. Stifled a gasp. The dark figure that stopped her in the hall was right behind her. Allison sucked in a frightened breath.

"Dad?"

The dark figure said nothing. It wavered, its form pliable. Then it moved. It grabbed Allison and punched her belly. She cried out, but her screams went unheard. Bill was trapped, upstairs, in his Scotch coma.

*

Back in Tamara's mother's room, the candle had found even more potency. Tamara radiated in the light of its yellow glow. The heat was causing small beads of sweat to form on her temples.

Tamara felt beautiful again. Maybe it was her mother's words or maybe it was the fact that she was about to attack. But she felt gorgeous. The girl in the dream who fucked Bill was back. She heard her father drunk and snoring and she laughed. It was as if the more the flame increased, the more power she attained.

"For this, I offer up my heart, my soul. My blood. I spill it in your name," she said.

Then she pulled out a small knife. And she cut her wrist.

*

Allison, screamed again, and reached for a butcher knife from the cutlery rack. She grabbed it and began swinging at the assailant in the dark. The blows to her stomach left a throbbing pain.

She yelled as she swung the shiny blade.

And then something grabbed her by the wrist. She dropped the knife. Her hands trembled. She shrieked again.

"Babe. It's me." Allison recognized the voice.

"Bill." She melted into him. He wrapped his arms around her and reached out and turned on the light. Allison saw that the kitchen was empty, excluding the two of them. She buried her face in his chest and started crying. "I was walking and someone grabbed me."

"It was a nightmare." Bill said, making sure his voice was soothing.

"It felt so real. I thought I saw my father. And he was trying to hurt our baby. All the Jung I studied and I still I don't know what it means." Bill took her chin in his hand and kissed her.

"Allison, of course on the day you find out we're having a child, you'd have a freak out nightmare."

"You think that's all it is?"

"I know that's all it."

Allison nodded. Desperate to believe him.

*

In Tamara's room, she felt like a failure again. The spell specifically said that the blood from the one requesting love had to pour, but, she'd only managed to break the skin. The pain of the cut was too much for her; she couldn't go through with it. So only a tiny drop of blood was mixed with the spell and the handkerchief. Tamara climbed into bed. Disgusted she couldn't find the courage to go deep enough. She pulled up the blankets and hid her head under them, waiting for sleep to end yet another day of futility.

Chapter 7

Tamara had set her alarm for 7:00 AM, but when some new, generic pop song played, she slept through it. Three more songs, and yet still Tamara slept. Finally, her phone rang and she woke up, groggily. It was almost 11AM.

"Hello?" She asked in that sweet tone one uses when not sure if it's night or day.

"Babe," the male voice said. Faint static crackled on the line.

"Sorry?" she asked, rising up on her elbows. She felt a pain in her wrist. She could feel a throb in the one-inch wound where the knife had dug in.

"I'm sorry. I'm so sorry," the male voice said.

"Who is this?"

"Tamara. It's Bill."

"Who?"

"Mr. Natolly."

Tamara grabbed her wrist, nearly dropping the phone as she did, and looked over at her book that was sitting on her desk. Maybe she had used enough blood after all.

"It doesn't sound like you," Tamara said.

"It's a bad connection. And I've been up all night. I had a huge fight," he said.

"With Allison?" Tamara rubbed her wrist and held back a smile.

"Yeah. I want to see you."

"But you can't."

She could hear her father, still snoring loudly, still sleeping in the hallway from his own excess.

"I can and you can. The Jackson Hotel. Tonight at 9:30."

"I don't know if my dad will let me," Tamara said.

She heard him snore again.

"Tamara I told you that you would meet someone who was perfect, whom you deserved. I think that person is me. Tonight. 9:30. The Jackson Hotel. Do you need money for a cab?"

Tamara knew her father's wallet would be safe to dip in to as he slept it off.

"You'd give me money for a cab?"

"Tamara, I think I love you. I'd give you anything you need."

"Mr. Natolly, you sound odd. Weird."

"I feel odd and weird. I feel like I'm about to finally get what I've always wanted," Bill said. And then, he added the words that Tamara had wanted to hear for months: "You."

"Really, Mr. Natolly?"

"Tamara?"

"Yes. Call me Bill from now on."

"Okay. Bill," she started to say, but before she could finish her thought, the phone died. She wasn't sure if it was his or hers and she didn't care. She looked over at her mother's book. It had worked.

"I can't believe it," she said.

She got up from her bed and twirled around like some ballerina in a Christmas pageant. It worked. She was going to get Bill. She dressed quickly and put her hair up. She started to leave the room, but halted, being sure to hide the spell book under her mattress first. Her father was lying on his stomach, his face turned and butting up against the floorboard. Tamara straddled him and carefully slid his wallet from his back pocket. She took out thirty dollars. Tonight, she told herself, was going to be the perfect night.

*

"You're evil," Kisha said as Shawn hung up the phone in his room. It oozed machismo. Trophies, posters of hot girls offset by a few of Derrick Rose and Peyton Manning. Shawn went over to Peyton's poster and tore it down.

"Babe, it could still happen." Kisha said. But they both knew he'd never be a poster on some kid's wall or have the jersey with his number on it that kids wore proudly to school. That dream was over.

"Tamara's getting what she deserves," he said back to her. "Now get over here and finish what you started."

Kisha grinned. She walked to him and got on her knees.

*

Evening had fallen and Tamara did something she never did. She opened her mother's closet and let her gaze purvey the numerous garments her mother used to wear. There was the emerald dress she always wore on St. Patrick's Day, in homage to her Irish roots. And the red dress she wore on Saturday nights, an homage to making her husband happy. But it was the black dress Tamara remembered the most. Her mother wore that as casually as most women wore a pair of jeans and in Tamara's mind, she never looked sexier. Casual, perfect, just enough skin, but never too much. The staple every woman should own.

She took it off the hanger and went over to the vanity. She undressed and put it on. It didn't quite fit her right, a little too big. But it worked well enough. Then she opened her mother's dresser drawer. She took out her makeup, which was remarkably still viable, and applied it. She did it all wrong. Her lips too red, her eyes too crusted with eyeliner, but she loved it. She loved the fact she looked like a woman, even if she only looked like a girl trying to be a woman.

"Still in here?"

Tamara turned around and saw her father. He had a beer in his hand, but hadn't officially started his next drunk cycle, so he wasn't that bad. Yet.

"And wearing you mother's clothes?" He was softer than last night. It was almost as if he was paying her a compliment.

"Yeah, some girlfriends invited me to a party and I thought I'd wear this. Is that okay?"

"A party? With actual people?"

"Dad."

He moved to her, putting the beer down on the desk near the books of witchcraft.

"I remember this dress. I remember her wearing it," he said, not able to hide his melancholy.

He leaned in and breathed, searching for some residual scent of the woman he loved.

"It still smells like her."

Then he grabbed Tamara like a stuffed animal and pulled her into him. Despite her initial trepidation, Tamara wrapped her hands around him and hugged him for the first time in a long time. For a moment it felt wonderfully paternal. But the hug lasted just a bit too long. Then she felt his hands move down from her shoulders and stroke the small of her back. There was nothing paternal about his touch now. Tamara had felt this touch from him before. After her mother died. Her stomach knotted. She pushed him away.

"I should finish getting ready."

Her father eyed her. Conflicting emotions flickered across his face. A hint of desire. Guilt. Self-loathing. He finally spoke. "Don't get in any trouble."

"I won't."

He leaned in to kiss her forehead, but stopped when she flinched. He looked down. Left without a word. Tamara shook off her unease and looked back in the mirror. She was all dolled up. And it didn't matter if she wasn't perfect. She felt beautiful.

Chapter 8

The parking lot of the Jackson Hotel, well, motel, was off Glenhaven Street. It was in the middle of the town, but there were no Cadillacs or BMWs in the parking spots. Beat up vans and old station wagons littered the cracked pavement. The Jackson Hotel was definitely not the Ritz.

"Where is he?" Roger asked Kisha and Shawn.

"Quit acting like this your first hotel party," Kisha said, knowing full well that was true. "Remember, Patrick is a very, very slow boy."

Shawn said, "He's popped more freshman cherry in this place than anyone. In history." As he said that, a working girl with a too tight shirt, and too short skirt, stumbled out the front door, teetering in her cheap heels. "And that's saying a lot."

Shawn and Kisha laughed as the woman dug in her bag for a cigarette. Roger looked on with the curious fascination. This was a new world for him.

As if on cue, Patrick emerged right after the prostitute had driven off in her old Tercel. He waved the three of them over.

"Got two rooms at half price," Patrick said as they approached. "Phase One is complete."

"Don't be a douche," Shawn said.

"This was your idea," Patrick said with a shrug.

"Wait. Why are we getting two rooms?" Roger asked. Shawn and Patrick gave each other fleeting, worried looks, but Patrick put out his hand.

"Roger, Roger, Roger. Ever heard of exotic dancers? They're gonna be in one room. Hopefully with you. The classy girls will be in the other room, hopefully with me." He paused. "Actually, maybe I'll take the first room," then he patted Roger on the back and the four of them walked into the lobby.

"Shit," Roger said to Shawn, "the video equipment you wanted is in the car."

"So let's go get it," Shawn said.

*

Tamara was back in her own room, finishing up her hair. It was too teased, but like her makeup, she loved it. She reached over to the vanity and kissed her own image. Then she grabbed the spell book she'd used last night and examined it before she tore out the love spell and tucked it in her pocket. She wanted to keep it close. Fearful that separation would weaken its magic. And she was too close to finding happiness to let that happen. Even if the happiness was created by magic.

Tamara left the house. But for the first time, it wasn't for school or on some stupid errand for her father. It was for her own enjoyment. She nearly skipped down the stairs and didn't even say goodbye to her father, who was cursing a bad throw on the television.

*

"I can't believe you're making me do this," Chloe said as they walked under the orange halo of a streetlight. "The Jackson Hotel? Where the dignity of good girls goes to die and the hormones of bad boys go to take it."

Jesse laughed.

"This is important to me. I told you. In LA, I was king. I need to reclaim my throne. Just a bit. And I have to do it with someone cool, like you. Besides, I couldn't come to my first party stag. Kind of ruins the whole idea of a kingdom," Jesse said, throwing his arms around Chloe.

"Oh, cue the end of your social life," Chloe said with a heavy eye roll. "Getting in with these douche-bags … not really the way to go."

"Forget them. We could get all kinds of crazy in a place like this," he said.

They reached the lobby and both noticed the faded carpet and the young receptionist, who was too busy texting to notice them.

"I mean all kinds of crazy," Jesse reiterated.

"You already said that. Are you flirting with me?" Chloe asked, and removed his arm from her shoulder with faux disdain.

"Stranger things have happened," Jesse said, trying to once again wrap himself around her.

The ruckus caused the receptionist to look up from her phone. She frowned. Quickly finished her text. And reluctantly, set the phone down.

"Room number?" She asked in a droll, bored tone.

"It's under Patrick, I'm guessing," Chloe said to the girl.

"Oh. Him. Room 19. As usual," then she picked up her phone and went back to her more important life, fingers blazing.

They walked down the long, carpeted hallway and knocked on the door to Room 19. Shawn opened the door and, inside, Chloe and Jesse saw Roger, who was drinking a beer, Kisha drinking a wine cooler, and Patrick drinking vodka straight out of the bottle.

"Shit," Jesse said. "We early? I should have known better. No good party starts on time."

Shawn, who was in host mode, gave them each a beer.

"We decided to keep this small," he said. "It's more like a pre-party."

"Yeah, next week is the all-out rager," Patrick added. "Parents are going to Fort Lauderdale for some convention. So Patrickpolooza Five is on, baby."

"That's what you call your parties? Seriously?" Chloe asked annoyed. She clearly wanted to be anywhere but there. Jesse shot her a look with a puppy dog face, begging her to play along. "Great!" Chloe said with forced enthusiasm. "We'll totally be there. In '90s clothes. I'll go as Anthony Kiedis. Jesse as Eddie Vedder. You know, when Lollapolooza was relevant."

"You're funny," Patrick said and took a pull off his vodka. He handed them the bottle of Smirnoff. "Shots!"

They each did one. Jesse left Chloe and Patrick and headed towards Roger, who was sitting on the bed alone.

"How goes it bro?" Jesse asked.

"Just enjoying the libations."

"Libations?"

"Beer," Roger said, realizing his geek-speak didn't work around cool people from Los Angeles. Or anywhere.

"Well, sounds like from your slightly slurred speech and ten dollar word, I have some catching up to do." Jesse downed his beer in one, long swill, and reached into the cooler for a second one. Roger tried to take two gulps of his beer and almost spit it out. While Jesse was in the running for kingship, Roger wasn't even at the table.

Patrick came over to them and nudged Jesse.

"You tapping that?" he asked, and looked over at Chloe, who was chatting with Kisha. Jesse turned bright red. Even kings had their weaknesses.

*

Across the room, Kisha put her hand on Chloe's shoulder.

"I'm sorry about the gym. I was in total mean girl mode," Kisha confessed.

"It happens. Apology accepted. I just think you're too hard on Tamara. The article she wrote, she didn't mean for it to get published. You should cut her some slack. She's nice. And girls like her ... well, they don't really have a chance at, well, anything."

Kisha did not want to have this conversation, so she quickly changed the subject.

"So, you and Jesse?"

"Friends," Chloe said, stopping Kisha in her tracks.

Kisha looked over at him.

"That boy can't take his eyes off you."

Chloe looked over at Jesse and Kisha was right. His eyes were stuck on her like the proverbial white on rice.

"Just grab me a wine cooler. Have any strawberry flavor? This beer is horrible."

*

Roger, still in awe at Jesse's beer drinking prowess, and even more in awe over Patrick's vodka guzzling, finally managed to finish his first beer. He held it up like a trophy and when he did, a small scar on his wrist was easily seen. Jesse noticed it, but didn't say anything. Shawn and Patrick were none the wiser.

"Roger! My man. Party fucking animal," Patrick said. "I'm getting you another one. I knew there was a reason we invited you to hang out with the cool kids. Might have to make you one of my Jackson Hotel road dogs."

"Really?" Roger asked.

"Really. Now take this bottle of vodka and do three pulls."

Roger eyed the bottle with trepidation. But he did it.

"Road dogs?" he asked Patrick.

"Road dogs, bro," Patrick said. As he took back the bottle, he noticed Shawn staring at his watch.

"Phase Two?" Patrick asked.

Shawn mouthed the word "douche" to Patrick. But then he nodded, smiled and the two high-fived.

"I got more booze in the car. Be right back," Shawn said. Before he left, Shawn grabbed the digital video camera and cord that Roger had brought from his A/V Club. No one noticed this; the girls were too busy talking about boys and the boys were too busy trying to out king each other with beer and vodka.

*

Tamara rode the crosstown bus in all of her beauty school dropout glory. She felt the stares and looks of the overweight bus driver, the schizophrenic who spoke of wild winds that were breaths of God, and the two Mexican maids gossiping in broken English. And she loved it. The night wasn't that cold. She could even spot Venus in the western sky. She had never felt happier.

*

When Shawn came back, through adjoining room 18, only Patrick noticed the black chord that now ran under the door. And saw Shawn fiddle behind the TV for a moment. The others were getting too drunk to care. They also didn't notice, he didn't bring back more alcohol. If anyone had asked, Shawn wouldn't have divulged his true mission. He had been in the next room. He'd set up the digital camera: its red light revealed it was on, hidden by a plant, in room 18. Then he connected it to the TV in Room 19. It took him all of five minutes.

"I need a drink, bitches," Shawn said. Roger threw him a cold one from the cooler.

*

The bus dropped Tamara off two blocks away from the Jackson Motel. She could see the yellow lights of the neon sign blinking on and off in the distance, the "J" fading in and out, like a lazy eye not sure if it was ready to blink. The wind swept up a bit and she grabbed onto her hair, fearing it might take it away. Take away her beauty and take away Bill. Leaves cartwheeled down the street and for some reason, this actually calmed Tamara's nerves. It made her feel like magic was everywhere, in the simplest events and movements.

As she entered the lobby, the receptionist was still texting away. Even though Tamara knew the room number, she wanted to be sure.

"Excuse me?" Tamara asked.

The girl looked up and faked a smile.

"Bill Natolly's room?"

"18." The girl looked at Tamara and shook her head. "He told me to give you the key." The girl handed it to her. "Good luck girlfriend."

"Thanks."

She walked down the hallway and her heart fluttered. It ebbed and flowed and dipped and darted. She breathed heavy. At the door, at Room 18, she traced the gold numbering. She straightened her dress and slid the plastic key into the small slot. She sucked in a nervous breath and opened the door.

*

Roger, Jesse and Patrick started a drinking game. They had to do a shot every time one of them said the word "the." They were all beyond fucked up in no time. Shawn, meanwhile, turned on the TV.

"What's that?" Chloe asked.

On the screen was just darkness.

"It's a movie," Shawn said. He went over to Kisha and kissed her.

"But there's nothing there."

"It's an indie film. Very Sundance."

Tamara entered the room to find it pitch black, save for two lit candles. She heard the shower running. On the table, next to a dozen red roses, was a note:

Get undressed, Tamara, I'm just cleaning up. Bill.

She went to the bed and found rose petals on the comforter and pillows. Her heart swelled.

She let her hands wash over the flames of the candles and in her mind she knew that magic worked. The heat of the flame not only didn't bother, it excited her.

She began to take off her mother's simple black dress. First over one shoulder and then her other. It fell to the floor.

"Shit, the exotic dancers!" Roger said with virgin excitement as the black TV showed the naked body in Room 18.

"You said 'the,' SHOT!" Patrick said.

The girl on the TV crawled out of her bra and panties too.

"What is this, public access?" Chloe said.

"Better. It's live entertainment," Patrick told her.

Chloe scoffed at the nude girl. It seemed forced. Like she was trying to prove her indifference. But Roger and Jesse were anything but indifferent.

"No one did stuff like this in LA," Jesse said. "You Midwesterners can party."

"Where's Shawn?" Chloe asked, realizing he wasn't there. "I'm sure he'd love this."

Tamara laid naked on the bed and listened to the water from the shower. The anticipation of it stopping, of seeing Bill wet and naked, was driving her insane. She reached up and caressed her breasts, for just a second. She could smell the subtle aroma of the roses and it made Tamara think about what her father had told her he loved most about her mother's favorite perfume. It was like springtime come to life.

The water turned off. Tamara trembled.

From behind the bathroom door, the voice told her to get on her knees.

"Bill?" she asked. Despite her hesitation, she instantly slid off the bed.

"Yes. It's what I like. Get on your knees, close your eyes and crawl to me."

Tamara giggled. But she did it. She got on her knees and closed her eyes and crawled to the man she loved.

When she found him, her hands flailed a bit in the dark as she rubbed up and down his legs.

"Tell me who loves me," the male voice said.

"Me. I love you, Bill," Tamara said.

"Then suck," he said. "Keep those eyes closed you beautiful thing. But suck."

She made her way up his leg and felt his dick. Her hand began to slightly jack it off. Her knees were burning a bit from the carpeting, but she didn't mind.

She started to put her lips around the head and then she heard the laughter. It confused her at first. But it was definitely laughter. Cruel laughter.

"Bill?" she asked, still obeying his orders of keeping her eyes closed. She reached for him, but the sturdy legs she was just rubbing were gone.

"Bill?"

Then the lights came on.

Tamara opened her eyes and looming over her wasn't Bill. It was Shawn. And he was recording everything. The camera stuck to his eye, the lens focused on Tamara's naked body, hunched over on all fours.

"Like I'd ever let your nasty mouth near my dick," he told her.

*

Patrick and Kisha roared with laughter from the other room, as they watched Tamara's foray into amateur porn.

"Is that, that girl from school?" Jesse asked.

"I thought you said it was a dancer." Roger said confused.

"Oh. My. God," Chloe said as the realization of what was happening slammed in to her like a freight train.

But no one could turn off the TV. It was a train wreck in the worst and best way. Shawn continued filming in Room 18.

"You ruined my life. Now I'm going to ruin yours. Welcome to reality TV. I would say you're going to be a star, but with that face … not so much."

Tamara sprung up from the ground and ran to the bed; Shawn stayed close behind.

"Where's Bill?" she asked as she found her mother's black dress and tried her best to put it on.

"You think Bill, or anyone, would do all this for you? Roses and shit? You look like some cheap whore."

"I don't understand." Tamara said.

"So, you're stupid too," he said, almost as an aside.

Tamara pulled on her mom's dress, but her naked face was distraught.

"Why?"

"Because you're a worthless human being Tamara," Shawn said.

She began to cry. Her whole body dropped the way age drops a face. Unfair and cruel. The kids watching it on the other TV all had different reactions. Patrick continued to laugh. Kisha stopped laughing and guilt started to creep across her face. Jesse and Roger felt they were being pranked. Chloe was pissed.

"Where is she?" Chloe asked.

No one answered.

Then Tamara's cries became wails echoing through the TV and walls.

Where the hell is she?"

Kisha looked at the TV. Her guilt in full bloom.

"She's next door. With Shawn."

"You all planned this?"

"Of course we planned it," Patrick said. "I say we do a shot for a job well done."

"I didn't know," Roger sputtered.

"You fuckers are sick," Jesse said.

Chloe leapt up from the couch and ran to the hallway. As she did, she met Tamara, who was doing her own running.

"You?" Tamara yelled.

"God no. I had no idea," Chloe responded.

"I trusted you. You're one of the only people I've ever trusted."

Behind Chloe, Jesse, Patrick, Kisha and Roger had entered the hallway.

"Great show, Tam!" Patrick said. The others remained perfectly silent.

Tamara shook her head. Her face grew dark. Like a wave of damned emotions was about to crash. "I've been through hell … my whole life. And you all, you live in dollhouses, and I'm stuck in a shed in the woods with nothing but shit."

Then Tamara did something she'd never done in her life. She screamed. She shrieked so loud, it seemed destined to wake the dead. And she wouldn't stop. And then she did something else she never did. She attacked. Chloe was her first victim. Tamara reached for Chloe, grabbed her by the throat, picked her up and began choking her.

"Tamara, stop," Jesse said, trying to protect the girl he was falling for. Tamara dropped Chloe to the ground, who gasped for air, then she attacked Jesse, scratching him on the neck, clawing his face, drawing blood that dribbled down his perfect Emo face.

Tamara spun to the next nearest warm body, Roger. He stumbled back into Room 19, as Tamara lunged at him. Forcing him onto the bed. Tamara leapt on him. Pummeling him.

The kids rushed into the room. Shawn dropped the camera to the carpeted floor. He grabbed Tamara and pulled her off Roger. She was in a frenzy. Blindly kicking and screaming.

"We need to shut her up," Shawn said.

Patrick took the lead and put one hand over her mouth and his second over her eyes.

"Don't hurt her," Chloe said, rubbing her sore throat.

But Tamara was doing most of the hurting. Finally. She bit down hard on Patrick's hand.

"Bitch," Patrick said as he let her go.

"Tamara, please. This wasn't—" But Tamara wasn't listening. She was wild and enraged and wanted nothing more than to hurt every single one of them. She took a few steps back and found herself entangled in the cord that Shawn set up so the others could see him film her degradation.

Her feet got tied up in the small rat's nest, and Tamara tripped. As she fell back, her head hit the edge of the heavy oak TV stand. The snap of her neck was audible. Her small body, in that little black dress her mother loved, dropped to the ground. Her face landed directly in front of the video camera. Her wide, glazed eyes reflected in its lens.

"Tamara!" Chloe said as she rushed to her.

Jesse knelt down beside her. "Is she okay?" he asked.

Chloe put her finger on the side of Tamara's neck. Her hands trembled.

"No pulse."

"Move over, my dad's a doctor," Kisha said. She, too, felt for a pulse. And then she started shaking Tamara's body. "Tamara, get up. Get up."

"Dad must be a shitty Doc," Patrick said.

Tears streamed down Chloe's face as she tried to calm herself. Shawn moved forward and shoved the girls out of the way.

"Get back, both of you," he said as he crouched over Tamara's body and grabbed her wrist. After a tense moment, he pulled back, as if he had touched a scalding teapot.

"Shit," was all he could muster.

"She's dead, isn't she?" Chloe said.

All five terrified kids looked at Tamara's body. They noticed a trickle of blood that seeped from the back her head.

"Oh God," Chloe said, and then she started weeping.

"No, no, no," Roger said.

Chloe pulled out her cell, but Shawn ripped it from her hand.

"Give me back my phone, Shawn," Chloe demanded.

"Let's just think about this, Chloe" Shawn said, as he held her phone up above his head, much too high for Chloe to reach.

"What's to think about? She's dead. We need to call the cops," Chloe said in between sobs.

"How will that help? You can't save the dead," Shawn said.

"Maybe they can revive her or something," Chloe said.

"They can't," Kisha said. "My dad really is a doctor and she's gone."

All five of them took awhile to allow this truth to sink in.

"We'll figure this out," Shawn said.

Roger, in his meekest tone, finally said what the others had been thinking: "We killed her. We all fucking killed her."

"No we didn't. She tripped and hit her head. Total accident," Shawn said.

"I second that," Patrick said.

The room was filled with more depression than mania. Roger sat down on the floor and put his hands over his eyes.

"We do the right thing and call the cops," Chloe said. "Give me my phone."

"I already have a record. I'll be put away for years," Patrick said. No one dared asked why he had a record.

"We all have lives. Kisha will be pre-med. Chloe, you said you're gonna go to art school and change the world. Jesse? I don't know you, but I'm sure you have things you wanna do with your life. I know I'm not throwing my life away because of her. No one knows she was here. She doesn't have any friends. Her dad's a useless drunk. We keep our mouths shut. People will think she ran away. No one has to know."

"Are you fucking out of your mind?" Chloe said.

"Shawn, we have to say something," Kisha added. "Her body and her blood are here. Forensics will find it."

"I can fix this," he said, his conviction strong.

"No. Give me my phone. Now," Chloe demanded. She lunged for the phone. Shawn shoved her away and Jesse, finally manning up, punched Shawn in the jaw. Shawn laughed. Football had taught him to take a punch. He went to the camera and took out the memory card.

"You stupid shits. You struggled with her. I got it all on Roger's equipment."

Roger blanched. "You asked me to bring it," he said. Shawn sneered, "Prove it." He turned to Chloe and Jesse, his voice deadly serious as he said, "You call the cops and I'll say you two set this all up. No one knows I'm even here. I'm off scot-free. But you guys? Fucked."

"You'd do that?" Chloe said.

"You'd be surprised what I'd do. And video doesn't lie. You two, and Roger, were fighting her." Shawn's steely gaze went to Roger.

"I have a scholarship to Duke," Roger whispered. "I'd lose it. I'd lose everything."

"We have her blood on us, Chloe," Jesse said in resolute sadness. "Scratches." Chloe shook her head in disgust at Jesse.

"Kisha?" Chloe said. But Kisha didn't respond. She shoe-gazed, afraid to make eye contact with anyone.

"I can't believe what I'm hearing," Chloe said.

"It's four against two, Chloe," Shawn said. "Actually, it seems like it's five against one."

"Jesse, we can't do this," Chloe urged.

"I don't like this any more than you, but it would be us against them and it sounds like everyone would make sure we took the fall."

Chloe looked to each of the other five. All she got was vacant stares.

The blood that had seeped out of Tamara's head was growing into a puddle.

Roger went to the window to open it and the wind blew in, the same wind that had blown the leaves down the street as Tamara stepped out of the bus. When he opened the window, he knocked over Tamara's purse. It fell to the floor, near her damaged head. The purse was unzipped. The lipstick tube fell out.

And so did the parchment that had the spell on it. Without anyone noticing, the brittle paper came to rest in the pool of Tamara's blood. It quickly became soaked in deep crimson. The small nick she'd done the previous night to get Bill to love her was a raindrop compared to the ocean of red that now engulfed the spell. Her blood had now truly been spilt for the man she loved.

"Close the window," Shawn said. Roger did as he was told.

"What do we do now?" Kisha asked.

"Yeah Shawn. What's your fucking plan?" Chloe said. She couldn't help but look at Tamara's dead body and as she did, she saw Tamara's eyes pop open. A dead, cold stare. Behind Tamara's head, Chloe momentarily noticed the parchment, but could only focus on Tamara's eyes. Chloe pointed, her mouth dropped, and she was about to say something when Tamara's eyes closed. Chloe went silent, sure her guilt addled mind was playing tricks on her.

Chapter 9

A few miles from the hotel, down a dusty road that veered off from the main highway, a car was parked near a fallen pine tree. Twenty yards away, in a small clearing, Patrick and Shawn were digging a shallow grave. The night had turned cold.

"Anyone have a jacket?" Roger asked.

No one answered.

"Fine. But you got all my stuff out of the room, right?"

"We got everything out, Roger. And cleaned the blood," Kisha said.

"Let's just finish digging," Shawn said. "No one comes out here—"

"Sometimes I bring girls here, when I can't afford a room," Patrick said. Shawn stared at him and shook his head.

"Who the fuck cares? None of us ever comes here again," Shawn continued and then waited until Patrick nodded in acquiescence. "And we never talk about what happened tonight."

Chloe looked at Tamara's body, which was slumped in the dirt. She didn't want to, but she couldn't help herself. She bent down and removed a loose strand of hair that was clinging to Tamara's face. And then it happened again. Tamara's eyes opened. Chloe fell backwards with a startle.

"Chloe?" Jesse asked, helping her up. "You okay?"

Chloe looked down at the corpse. Tamara's eyes were closed.

"Guys, we have to call the police. It was an accident. Roger, you will still get into Duke. Kisha, you will still be pre-med. I don't care about me. Patrick? Fuck you."

"And me?" Shawn said.

"I'll take care of you," Kisha said. Shawn rolled his eyes and turned to Chloe. "It isn't happening. So drop it," Shawn said and continued digging. Jesse wrapped his arms around Chloe.

"It's all gonna work out," Jesse said.

He said that exact same refrain again, a half-an-hour later, when Shawn and Patrick pushed Tamara's body into the hole in the ground and covered her with dirt. Through the rows of conifers, the sickle moon found an entrance and cast a silvery shadow over the newly minted grave.

Chapter 10

Chloe arrived home. She didn't greet her mother. She didn't check her email. Or grab a quick bite. She went straight to her room, undressed and crawled into bed. It felt as if this singular night was actually eternal. She clutched her pillow and waited for sleep to overtake her. When it did, she didn't see darkness or those strange astral menageries at the onset of dreams.

She saw Tamara.

Chloe was back in the pines standing over Tamara's shallow grave. Wind gusted. Moonlight split the darkness. Chloe stared at the mound of dirt. The dirt that covered the sins of her and the others kids.

Suddenly, the earth heaved and Tamara rose up from her wooded grave like an evil phoenix. She shoved Chloe to the ground.

"The fuck?" a voice said. Chloe turned back and saw the other kids standing behind her. Kisha huddled against Shawn. Jesse, Patrick and Roger stood in impotent fear.

Tamara, her hair wild and black, stared at her former tormentors.

"Tamara?" Chloe asked wearily.

Tamara cocked her head for a moment, as if examining a strange new species. Then she attacked Shawn with a demon's strength. She bit in to his face, jerked back and tore out a chunk of his cheek. Patrick grabbed Tamara. She spun towards him. Spit out the meaty piece of Shawn's neck she held in her mouth. She reached out, lightning fast, and grabbed Patrick's throat. Ripped it out and blood flowed like a sacrifice. It sprayed Kisha. She started to scream, but Tamara swiped out, raking her nails across Kisha's face. Shredding her beauty in the blink of an eye. Kisha fell to the ground and clutched her face as blood streamed through her fingers.

Roger and Jesse backed away from Tamara.

"Tamara, stop this," Chloe said. "This isn't you."

"Tamara's dead. I'm something else now," As Tamara uttered these words, Chloe noticed that the forest went quiet as a tomb. The tall trees had no wind to sway in. The raccoons and skunks and whatever other creatures lurked in the shadows stayed far away from this place.

Tamara turned to Roger. Roared at him. Roger fell to his knees in fear.

"Please," he pleaded, "I was tricked."

Tamara smacked Roger across the face, knocked him to the ground. Tamara put her foot on Roger's head.

"No," Chloe said.

Tamara smiled at Chloe. A twisted smile that said all of Tamara's humanity was gone. She pressed down with all her might. Roger's bones cracked and his head caved as Tamara ended his life. Chloe screamed. Snapped awake. She hoped, actually prayed, she would be in her bed. But she found herself back in those pined woods.

This dream played out on a loop throughout the long night. Chloe tossed and turned in her small twin bed, until the morning sun began to shine. Its amber light illuminated a girl's room. But instead of ponies and teen-dream pinups, Chloe's room was anything but typical. A Scarface poster and a framed autograph of Scarlett Johansson as Black Widow hung from the wall. Clothes were strewn about. An Xbox controller was in knots on the floor.

Like her room, Chloe, in her slumber, was not acting like a typical teenage girl.

"No, no, Tam, no," she muttered. Her voice seemed to get louder and louder as dawn become morning. Finally, Chloe's mother, dressed in a conservative pantsuit, flung open her daughter's door, ran to her and shook her awake.

"Baby," Chloe's mom said.

Chloe shot up. The surroundings, the same ones she'd lived in her whole life looked foreign and strange.

"Honey, that's some nightmare you're having."

"Uh, it's nothing," Chloe responded.

"That wasn't nothing. Sounded like a freakin' horror fest."

Chloe tried to muster a laugh.

"It was a horror fest. You tried to make me wear a dress to school." Her mother looked at her, not believing her. Then she spied something on Chloe's neck. A bruise.

"Where'd you get that?"

"Mom. You know I'm klutz central. I tripped running in gym class."

"Really?"

"Sadly, yes. Embarrassing, I know. Thank god I have these brooding good looks." Her mother bought it.

"Well, I made eggs and bacon. I have to run into the office for a weekend meeting. Talk about a nightmare," her mother said as she walked to the door. "Get up and get some food. You were out late last night. The party that good?"

"It was okay."

"Be honest. Did you drink?"

"One beer. One vodka shot."

"I'd rather it be nothing. But thanks for telling me."

Her mother looked at her again.

"Sweetie, that thing on your neck? It looks like a handprint."

"Nope. Just a fall on gravel. You're tripping. Like people who see the Virgin Mary in toast. Lucky fall." Chloe laughed. So did her mother.

"Come down before the eggs get cold." Then she blew a kiss in her daughter's direction and left the room.

After her mom closed the door, she looked at the bruise in the closet mirror. It was a handprint. Tamara's. She put her own hand on the mark and then fell back into her bed and wept for what she'd done.

*

School started on Monday. Chloe passed Kisha and Shawn in the hall, and even though it was Tamara who'd died, they all seemed like creatures from beyond the grave. No one said a word to anyone. Complexions were white and waxy.

Jesse came up to Chloe and gently put his arm around her. She pushed him away.

"Didn't see you in the quad today."

Chloe glared at him.

"I bought you some orange juice and a bagel."

She quit glaring, but still remained silent.

"Chloe, I wanted to bail too. I wanted to stay home. Hell, I wanted to buy a ticket back to LA."

Kisha and Shawn held hands as they walked further down the hall. When they turned a corner, Chloe took a breath.

"We have to be like them. We have to be normal. Or at least act normal," Jesse said. Chloe nodded with zero enthusiasm. Jesse reached into his book bag and pulled out the bagel.

"Extra schmere."

Chloe took the bagel, unwrapped the cellophane and took a bite. She forced it down.

*

"So, last week we talked about duality in literature. This week we are going to riff on that topic. Anyone care to guess?"

The class looked at Tamara's empty seat. She was the only one who would know this and they all knew it. Chloe touched her empty desk.

"Dichotomy."

"Aren't those, like the same thing?" Shawn asked.

"Some people think so. But others don't think duality is a choice. One can choose to be good or evil. But dichotomy seems almost like a psychotic break. Can anyone think of a great character in literature that isn't a dualist, but a dichotomist?"

No one said a word. Finally, Chloe raised her hand.

"Chloe?" Bill asked, almost surprised.

"Jane Eyre."

"How so?"

"She started off plain and then became better than her plainness. But she never lost her plainness. She just learned to outgrow it. Both still existed. The plainness and the belief in herself. She had to accept that both things were a part of who she was. And in something like Jekyll and Hyde, he could only be one or the other. He was stuck in duality."

Mr. Natolly beamed.

"Well done, Chloe."

"Can I use the restroom?" Chloe asked. Mr. Natolly waved her off, as if giving her a free pass for her spot on remark. She grabbed her purse and headed for the door.

As she left the class, she ran into the last person she'd ever thought she'd see.

Tamara.

Chloe almost passed out from fright. She dropped her purse. Tamara stepped on it and crushed its contents. The leftover bagel oozed out of the pocket.

"Hey Chloe!"

Chloe went pale. Tamara put her hand on Chloe's forehead.

"You coming down with something? You look like you've seen a ghost."

With Tamara's hand on Chloe's forehead, Chloe couldn't help but look at Tamara's face. It was, well, it was beautiful. Her acne was clear. The scar from her fall was gone. She'd thinned out, somehow. Her eyes looked like emeralds. Her lips pouted like Angelina Jolie's.

"Tamara," was all Chloe could say.

"Have to run. I'm already late for class. Go deal with your period or whatever." Chloe grabbed her fallen purse. And stood dumbfounded in the hall.

*

"Bill, sorry I'm late," Tamara said as she stood in the doorway leading into Mr. Natolly's English class. "Had a lot to deal with. Weekends. They can be rough and, I swear, this one nearly killed me."

Tamara sauntered into the room and made sure to give Jesse, Shawn, Kisha and Patrick a very knowing grin. She pulled down her little black dress, which had slid up her thighs. Patrick noticed her new and improved body and couldn't help but stare at her curves.

Tamara sat not at her own desk, but at Chloe's, who had come back to the room and was staring shell-shocked near the door.

"Bill, again, sorry I'm late. I actually read the very beginning of Proust's "Remembrances of Things Past." Do you know it's all about nothing? It's just about time. How it slowly goes on and on." Tamara laughed.

"Tamara, you missed a quiz. You'll have to make it up."

"And I will." She crossed her legs and she let Mr. Natolly gaze at what was underneath her mother's black dress.

"Well, okay, let's get back to the lecture," Mr. Natolly said and went to the dry erase board to start writing.

Sitting in front of Tamara, Jesse focused on a blank piece of paper, pretending to find meaning in the sea of white. His hands trembled.

"You okay, Jesse?" Tamara whispered in his ear. "You're shaking a bit."

"Fine," he mumbled, not taking his eyes of the paper.

Chloe had gathered herself and walked back towards the rows of desks. She sat at Tamara's old desk, near the back, where the posters on the wall said silly inspirational things about teamwork and trusting others and never giving up.

The tension in the room was palpable. The guilty kids exchanged terrified looks as Tamara glanced around and witnessed it, relishing in their obvious fear and confusion.

The bell rang.

"Quizzes on In Cold Blood are due. Please pass them forward," Mr. Natolly said. The students did as he instructed. But Tamara reached over to Jesse's paper, not the blank one, but the one with lines of writing on it, and grabbed it. He nearly leapt out of his chair.

"Come on Los Angeles boy," she whispered. "You came from the land of starlets to toy with, Sunset Boulevard to play on and clubs to get fucked up in. All of those things are scary to small time kids like us. But you managed. And my little touch scared you?"

"It, um, didn't-- " he said with a stutter. "I just, I wasn't expecting it."

"You're a smart boy and I don't want to take a makeup quiz." She held out her hand and her voice turned stern, "Give it to me."

Jesse gave her his paper. She scribbled out his name and added her own. Tamara stayed in her seat as the other kids left. She pretended to write in her notebook. Chloe, Shawn, Patrick and Jesse exited the room with their feet moving forward, but their eyes back on Tamara. She freaked them out. Simple as that.

With the classroom emptied, Tamara walked up to Bill. This time she didn't fix her dress, she let it ride up her thighs.

"Quiz is done."

"How? You just started it."

She handed Mr. Natolly Jesse's pilfered quiz.

"Capote knew nothing about murder, Bill. He just knew about obsession. It isn't hard."

"Tamara, I'd prefer you call me Mr. Natolly," he said, as he perused her quiz. "Are you okay?" he asked.

"No. I feel bad about last Friday," Tamara said.

Mr. Natolly breathed a sigh of relief.

"I was just feeling a bit awkward and down on myself. Silly girl stuff," Tamara said.

"Boys feel awkward and silly too, Tamara."

"You published something I didn't want you to. And it made me sort of love and hate you," she said.

"I'm sorry, Tamara. I really am. I just didn't think it through."

"I'm over it."

"So you're good?"

"I'm good, Bill."

"Tamara, I really think you should call me Mr. Natolly."

"You said that already," she said and smiled. "But I'm gonna call you what I want." She leaned in and ran her finger down Bill's button up shirt. She let it linger on his top button, undid it, then buttoned it up again.

"Oh and I'm better than good, Bill. I'm perfect."

And then she left the room. Mr. Natolly's eyes couldn't help but look at her ass. And it was a perfect ass.

*

In the hallway, where Tamara had once stared into the mirrored glass at the dream version of her imagined beauty, Chloe, Shawn, Jesse and Patrick walked like zombies. Kisha was talking to a cheerleader with frosted hair. Shawn ran up to her.

"Babe?"

"Hang on, I - - " she said, before Shawn grabbed her arm and pulled her away, mid-sentence.

He dragged Kisha into an empty room. The others joined them.

"She's alive." Shawn said.

"What?"

"Tamara's alive."

Kisha laughed. "Babe, that's not how anatomy works."

"We must have buried her alive," Chloe said. She flicked her fingers nervously. "We fucking buried her alive."

"Wait. You're being serious?" Kisha asked.

"No we didn't. She was dead," Shawn said, ignoring Kisha.

"As a doornail," Patrick added. "And today she doesn't have any scars. Or bruises. And what about how she looks?"

Kisha stared at the kids, her dark skin paled as this news sank in. "You're not joking. She's here?"

Chloe felt the bruise on her neck, which was still very real and painful. Jesse took her hand.

"She must have been unconscious," Jesse said.

"No way," Kisha said. "No fucking way."

They stopped talking, each trying to figure out exactly what to say, or do, next.

"I never told you guys, but my mom and her mom were friends," Patrick said. "Her mom was fucking crazy. Into all this insane witch stuff."

"What are you saying, Patrick?" Chloe asked.

"My mom, back in those days, was all into Wicca and shit. So was Tamara's mom. And so was Tamara."

"What does that have to do with anything?" Kisha asked.

"I'm saying that bitch is a witch," Patrick said.

"God, you're never getting out of high school, Patrick. Chloe is right. We fucked up. Buried her alive," Shawn said. Another wave of silence befell the group.

The bell rang. The kids sighed. The room, the silence of it, seemed liked some sort of sanctuary.

"History," Kisha said.

"Remedial Math," Patrick said.

"Free period. No more football," Shawn said.

"I have Physics. Tamara's in that class. I have to talk to her. Get to the bottom of this," Chloe said.

They opened the door and standing in the hallway was Mr. Natolly.

"Hey kids," he said. When he saw the five of them together, he cocked his head a bit. He knew Chloe would never socialize with at least three of them.

"Hey teach," Patrick said.

Bill walked down the hallway.

"I need to find Roger," Chloe said. "He has Physics with us. If I don't tell him and he sees her, he'll freak."

Bill watched curiously as the motley group continued to conspire. Then he saw Chloe walk away, scratched his head, shrugged his shoulder, and headed towards the teacher's lounge.

*

The A/V room was sadly sparse and dated. There were a few Macs and some editing equipment. Several large TVs were attached to clunky operating systems.

Shawn's last football game was playing on the large TV and Roger was haphazardly watching it, stopping it every now and then to make one of Shawn's errant throws miraculously disappear. What Roger loved most about this place was the large soundproof window that served as a barrier between the A/V room and the bustling hallway. In here, he could ignore all the white noise of high school and get lost in his thoughts. And focus on the work at hand.

Behind Roger was a wall with five monitors on it. Each displayed videos of school events that Roger was editing. Basketball games. The school play, a horrible rendition of Oklahoma where Kisha played the lead. Debate Club discussing the efficacy of drones. But Roger wasn't really watching any of it. He had a Bach sonata playing in the background and was reading the new Batman comic. The one where Batman was a teenager. Roger was desperately diving into the fantasy world of the Dark Knight to avoid the reality of his. To avoid the fact that he covered up the death of a girl even he, a nerd amongst nerds, never paid attention to.

Suddenly, the monitor that was playing Kisha's off pitch song, went black and a blood-curdling scream was heard. Roger dropped the Batman comic. He turned around. He heard the scream again. He had heard that scream before. In fact, he had heard it this past weekend.

"Tamara," he said.

He bolted up from his chair and studied the monitor. Kisha and her cowboy gear was gone. Another image appeared. It was the video of Tamara at the Jackson Hotel. Roger tried to turn off the monitor, but he couldn't. The button wouldn't work. He was forced to watch the nightmare of the weekend, all over again. Tamara's fight with Chloe and Tamara's assault on Jesse. He looked for a digital card in the computer console, but it was empty.

Panicked, Roger looked around. Outside, behind the soundproof wall, he saw Shawn and Kisha kissing against a locker. Thankfully no one was walking by. No one could see the horror playing on the monitors.

Now the glowing screen showed the events after Shawn set down the camera in Room 19.

Roger knew what was playing: the struggle moments before Tamara fell and hit her head. The struggle before Tamara died.

"Fuck," he said, realizing what this meant. Realizing that somehow, someone had made a copy of Shawn's recording.

And then it happened. After a deafening crack, then a brief moment of silence, Tamara's face slammed into view. The feet in the shot, his feet among others, blurred into obscurity. All the focus was on Tamara. Her eyes looked right at Roger and they were dead. Her pupils were large and midnight black and the thin layer of an emerald iris appeared dull and glazed.

Roger rose from his chair. He grabbed his heart and slowly backed up as those eyes of Tamara's watched him watching her. He bumped into the soundproof glass.

The audio was still viable, and Patrick was saying something stupid that Roger couldn't quite comprehend.

But he did hear Chloe's voice very clearly.

"She's dead, isn't she?" Chloe's voice said on the tape. Roger put his hand over his mouth and then a voice rang out from behind him.

"I don't know Rog? Am I?"

He spun around and went pale when he saw Tamara standing there.

"Tamara?"

"In the flesh."

"But, I. But, we."

"No wonder you never get laid. Words matter, kiddo."

"How?" Roger asked. Behind him, Kisha and Shawn were still making out. Now he hated that soundproof glass.

"Does it really matter how? Aren't you just glad to see me?"

"I, um, I."

"Roger spit it out," Tamara said and took her gum out and stuck it to the table.

"We didn't mean to. None of us meant to."

"I know, Roger. Things just got out of control. It was all my fault I tripped. Right?"

"No. What they did was horrible," he said, backing up.

"They?" Tamara began to walk towards Roger.

Roger didn't know what to say. He bumped into the desk, which meant no more room to backtrack. Finally, he found his words.

"You're okay. That's all that counts," he said, with a big, congenial smile.

Tamara laughed. "You really think I'm okay?" She took three methodical steps closer so that her face was right next to Roger's. "You think just because I look like this, I'm okay?"

Tamara's eyes narrowed. She ran her fingers through her hair.

"You buried me, Roger."

"We thought you were dead."

"Don't interrupt me," she instructed. Roger nodded in assent. "Do you have any idea what that feels like?"

"I'm so sorry. I—"

"What did I say about interrupting? Answer the question? Do you know. How it feels. To be buried. Alive?"

"No," Roger said.

Tamara let that sink in for Roger. She rolled her neck around like an athlete beginning to stretch.

"Well, today is your lucky day. I'm going to show you."

She steadied her face and locked eyes with Roger. He tried to look away but he couldn't, as if stuck in Medusa's trance. Tamara reached out and touched Roger's pimpled face. She rubbed her fingers up and down his cheeks and suddenly the images in this geek's mind changed from computers and video equipment to visions of Tamara's decayed face. Roger tried to close his eyes, but couldn't. Tamara had some kind of hold on him. He had no choice but to watch as Tamara's skin began to fall off her cheekbones.

"No," he said, over and over, to no avail.

Then the room began to change. It became a surreal dream instead of an outdated A/V haven, and the first thing that Roger saw, other than Tamara's rotted face, was a razor blade. It just appeared on the desk. And after that a bathtub appeared, right under the large video monitor. The tub was half-filled with lukewarm water and bubbling on the surface was what appeared to be a bottle of pills. Roger then saw someone, whose face was turned away, slouched over in the bathtub. The person's wrist was exposed. And the water, which was rising towards the lip of the tub, was turning a deep red.

Roger shook himself out of the dream. He screamed. The images disappeared. Things were back to normal. A tear rolled down his face. Tamara wiped the tear from his cheek and stuck it in his mouth. He was back under Tamara's spell and he swallowed the tear. The images came instantly back, the tub, the slouched bather, the blood.

"So let me show you what it's like to be buried alive. You wake up in the cold wet ground. Scared. Alone. You have no idea where you are. How you got there. You claw at the ground trying to find air or escape or anything that makes sense, when nothing makes sense."

She circled Roger like a lioness toying with a wounded impala.

"You claw so hard your hands bleed. But you know all about bleeding don't you?"

Roger looked down at his wrists, and somehow, blood was pouring down from them. He was able to say one word: "How?"

As the blood poured and poured, fountain-like, he looked at the bathtub. The person in the tub was him. Then his hands began to fold in on themselves from the lack of blood. The cuts widened. His sinews showed. Then his bones.

"You try to scream, underground, in the dirt, in the woods. But no one hears you. Not having a voice, Roger? It's painful, isn't it?"

Roger tried to scream. But only air came out.

"Let's be honest. You never really had a voice, did you Roger? You've been living under dirt your whole life."

Roger grabbed for his neck, trying to force out words. None came. In fact, all that did was a large puff of dirt.

Tamara smiled. "And in the dirt, there are bugs. Worms. They think you're a meal. And I sort of was, wasn't I? The circle of life, right?"

Roger gasped as he coughed up more dirt.

"The thing is, once the insects start burrowing into you, it's almost like the razor you used on your wrist. It hurts and all you want is for it to go away. But I couldn't go away. Flesh seems so tough, but really, it's incredibly easy to destroy."

Roger's eyes looked down and then he saw them. Night crawlers, beetles, cockroaches. They began crawling up his legs. He tried to swat them away, but his arms were paralyzed. The bugs crawled up his skin.

Tamara ripped off his jeans with her talon fingernails. He stood there in his underwear as the bugs crawled up his thin, pasty legs. And then they began to burrow into him.

"Oh God," he said.

"Now you can talk. Good," Tamara said.

"Please Tamara," he pleaded, still trying to kick off the insect attack.

The night crawler wormed its way into his shin, causing it to bleed. The cockroaches crawled up his arms and dug into the open wounds near his wrist, chewing on the exposed bones. The beetles found his mouth. They crawled into it and tore into his lips and tongue. His knees buckled. He fell to the floor. Tamara loomed over him.

"I think you get it now, Roger. I went through all of this because you were too afraid to stand up."

Then she released him from the spell and Roger curled in the fetal position on the floor. The bugs and the dirt and the bloody wrists all vanished.

"Please, no more. Please," he said. "I never thought it was going to be you. I didn't know. If I had, I would have stopped it."

"And that's supposed to make me feel better?" Tamara asked. "Everyone's right. You are a loser. And what would they think if they knew the whole truth? That you're a sad little boy with a scarred wrist and a small dick."

She tossed him his pants.

"You can't bleed the pain away Roger. Put on your pants."

Tamara looked at the monitor still that was still playing Shawn's football game. "I see you haven't finished editing that. See, that's your problem, Roger," she said. "You never finish what you start. A sentence. A clip of a game. And," she made a slicing motion across her wrist. "Nothing."

She began to walk away, but as she reached the door, she turned.

"If you want to be remembered for who you are after you die, you have do something unforgettable while you're alive."

*

Chloe and Jesse worked together dissecting a frog carcass.

"So, Tamara wasn't in Physics class," Chloe said.

"Well how'd your talk go with Roger?" Jesse asked. He split open the torso. Guts oozed out.

"I couldn't find him. Looked everywhere. He's never not shown up for Physics."

"Maybe he did what we should have done and just stayed home."

Chloe nodded. "Maybe."

The class monitor, one of the new modern conveniences the Board did approve, turned on and the teacher stopped the class.

"Looks like Principal Kendricks has an announcement. Everyone pay attention," he said. The kids seemed relieved to put away the innards of rotted amphibians.

"Good afternoon, Sebastian High," the voice said, but it didn't come from the bald, portly Mr. Kendricks. It was Roger.

"Shit," Chloe said. Roger's face on the screen seemed stoic and sad.

"I know a lot of you see me as some loser video game geek, with bad skin and an aversion to sunlight. Well, this weekend I did something horrible. It made me realize that all of you who ignored me and made me feel invisible were right. I'm a waste of space." Roger paused. His eyes found the floor.

Chloe and Jesse exchanged glances. Jesse reached out for Chloe's hand and she let him take it.

*

In history class Shawn and Patrick were also watching the monitor. They also gave concerned looks, but no hands were held.

Roger started to speak again. "Just like I'll never be anything more than an invisible human, I'll never be able to fix what I did. But I can try and make things right."

"He's gonna tell everyone, that dick," Patrick whispered. "I'm gonna kill him."

*

In Civics, Kisha bit her nails, watching Roger talk.

"Can we turn this off?" she asked her teacher.

Kisha's teacher simply shook her head. She, like the rest of the class, was riveted by what was happening.

"I can accept my punishment," Roger said on the screen.

*

Tamara walked down the hallway. She went to the glass case where Shawn's championship trophies were. She took her fist and busted through it. She took out the trophies and smashed them.

Then she began to mouth words. The words that Roger was saying. Tamara had taken total control of him. She was now his voice and his limbs.

In Mr. Natolly's class, he too was riveted by Roger. But something didn't feel right about what he was witnessing, like he needed to investigate.

"I'll be right back."

Bill walked down the hall to the A/V Center, where he knew Roger was. As he did, he heard Roger's voice echoing through the halls.

"I want to give all of you some advice. Never be afraid to stand up for what's right."

*

"Jesse, what's he doing?" Chloe whispered, "He'd never confess."

The dead frog reeked. Jesse pushed it as far away as he could.

"I don't know. Still waters run deep," Jesse said.

On the screen, Roger smiled.

"Don't sit in your little plastic houses wearing your cheap mall outfits and lie about who you are and what you really want."

Chloe took her hand away from Jesse. She clenched it into a fist. As she did, Roger left the frame for a moment. When he returned, he had an Exacto knife in his hand. He raised his hand to let everyone watching know the knife was going to be the star of this performance.

"First rule … hear no evil. So, all of you arrogant, self-involved brats who think the ugly, rejected, and tragically un-cool kids exist only for you to make fun of? This is for you."

Roger took the knife, placed it to his ear. Then slowly began to saw away at it. Slicing through the cartilage.

"Oh my God." Jesse said. Others moaned. A girl vomited as Roger cut off his ear. Instead of crying or wincing in pain, Roger grinned.

As the Van Gogh ear fell to the floor, Mr. Natolly reached the A/V center. He was shocked to see Roger standing in front of a camera, blood gushing from his ear. He began to pound on the soundproof glass. Beating it with all his might, but Roger didn't flinch.

In a few moments, Allison joined him. She too began beating the glass.

"What's going on?" she asked rhetorically.

"I don't know. But I have to get in there."

"I don't understand. Roger's the sweetest boy in school," Allison said.

"And we all know what comes next, don't we?" Roger said through the intercom. "This one is for you assholes who gossip or tell lies about everyone. Speak no evil."

Roger used the serrated blade to slowly and deliberately cut out his tongue. The limp organ fell out of his mouth like jelly to the floor.

"Bill! Get in there!" Allison screamed.

Bill ran across the hall and found a chair. He flung it against the glass pane of the door. Behind Bill, several other teachers joined him.

But Roger had one more thing to say. As well as someone can speak without a tongue.

"And por bose of us too unborthy of love and beauty? See no evil."

With angelic calm, Roger, in his final act, raised the knife high and jammed it down in to his right eye. It popped like a grape. Then, somehow, he did the same to his other eye. It all seemed too easy.

*

Chloe watched the TV screen, helpless, as Roger's destroyed body fell to the floor. The blood made Roger look like a pomegranate doll. Jesse couldn't look. In disgust, he pushed the dead frog over the edge of the desk.

In History class, Shawn and Patrick held hands. Bro hands. They said nothing.

In Civics, Kisha screamed.

Then the monitor went black.

Chapter 11

Bill leapt through the shards of glass after he was finally able to break through the barrier. He ran to Roger and knelt down. The knife was stuck in his left eye. Blood was everywhere. Allison moved right behind her husband.

"Bill," was all she could say. Roger's lifeless body looked smaller than ever. Bill got up and hugged his trembling wife.

*

Allison, now in serious counselor mode had a line of students waiting to speak to her. Two cops stood outside her door. Inside, Chloe sat with her arms crossed as Allison spoke to her.

"Chloe, why are you being evasive?"

"I just saw someone commit suicide."

Allison softened.

"Mr. Natolly overheard you say in third period that you needed to find Roger and tell him something. I don't think the two of you usually run in the same circles, do you?"

"What? Why are you asking me that?"

"It's just a simple question. You two don't, didn't, run in the same circles, did you?"

Chloe thought hard and fast.

"My friend, Jesse wanted this new video game, the newest Halo, and I wanted to ask Roger if I had the right one. But I never found him."

"Okay. Well if you ever feel any anxiety—"

"—I wish I'd found him. I wish I'd found him and maybe he wouldn't have done what he did."

"It's important that you don't blame yourself for this," Allison said.

But Chloe did. She shuffled in her chair. "I just want to go home," she said.

"Okay, sweetie. That's all for now. But if you ever need to talk I'm here. Okay?"

Chloe nodded and hurried out of the office. She was keenly aware of the other kids waiting in line to talk to Allison and even more keenly aware of the cops.

As she went down the hallway, she almost ran into Mr. Natolly.

"Chloe, you okay?" he asked.

She just shook her head.

He let her leave and walked into his wife's office.

"How bad is this?" he asked her.

"Really bad. I'm gonna be here all night. They need me."

"I wish I could help."

"Knowing you'll be home when I get there helps me. And that lets me help them."

"I'll get Kendricks to give me a ride home," he said, as he bent over her desk and kissed her. "I'm so lucky to have you and so are these kids."

"What a horrible day," she lamented.

Bill walked around the desk and talked directly to Allison's stomach.

"Luna. Your mom's gonna help these kids like we'd want someone to help you."

Allison grabbed her husband's hand and held it tight. Then she let it go.

"So dinner? Steak?" Bill asked.

"Pasta. Alfredo. Tons of cream," Allison said. "Comfort food tonight."

"So did you find out what Chloe said she needed to talk to Roger about?"

She shook her head.

"Jesse said she needed some computer science help from him. Shawn said he knew this freshman girl who thought Roger was 'Steve Jobs' hot and wanted to meet her. Patrick said he wanted to borrow money. Chloe said she wanted to learn about a new video game as a gift for Jesse. I guess Jesse and Roger were both gamers."

"I don't buy it," Bill said. "It's way too convenient that four kids with four different agendas all had to talk to him today. When I saw them huddled together, whatever they were discussing involved all of them."

"Well, I appreciate the diligent sleuthing, but first things first. I need to do my job and assess their immediate emotional needs," she said. "Oh, and babe, make some garlic bread, too."

Chapter 12

In the Sebastian High football field, underneath the rows of stained bleachers, Chloe, Shawn, Jesse, Kisha and Patrick gathered in an informal circle. It was a cool day and the sky was Southern California blue.

"I told Allison some girl wanted me to hook 'em up," Shawn said.

"I said I needed money." Patrick said. "Which really wasn't a lie."

"I told her I needed help with my computer science class," Jesse said.

"And I said I needed video game advice for you," Chloe said, looking at Jesse, who couldn't help but smile.

"So you all lied," Kisha said.

"We've been lying since this all started," Chloe said. "And this was amateur hour. We should have talked first, got our stories straight."

Kisha grabbed hold of the metal bar on the bleachers. "My dad says in times of extreme stress, PTSD can set in and people, in shock, can sort of lie. Get scattered. So if anyone asks again, just say you all wanted to talk to Roger about all those things. Just not today. That sounds too suspicious."

"Agreed," said Shawn.

Patrick, in a rare moment of mental acuity, simply said, "I can't believe he offed himself."

"If he knew Tamara was alive, I don't think he would have," Chloe said.

"There are a hundred 'ifs' that we could debate until we die. But you looked for him, Chloe. You couldn't find him. What he did isn't on you," Jesse said.

"He took the easy way out," Shawn said.

"No, we did," Chloe said. "Stop the mental gymnastics and fucking admit it. We took the easy way out."

From deeper under the bleachers, the group heard a voice.

"Oh guys, don't be so hard on yourselves. Accidents happen."

Tamara emerged from the shadows of the stands.

Shawn, Kisha, and Patrick backed away. But Chloe moved towards her. Jesse tried to grab Chloe's hand, but she wouldn't take it.

"Tamara, we have to talk about this," Chloe said.

"It's fun seeing you scared, Chloe. Insecure. A bit unsure. Not sure what's up, what's down. That's how I used to be. Totally sucks, right?"

"Like you said, accidents happen, right?" Kisha said.

"Shut up you bitch," Tamara said, her face hardening. Then she changed in a heartbeat. Smiled, a blindingly white pageant smile. "I should actually thank you. Now I know what I want and, more importantly, how to get it."

"Tamara, I had no idea what they were planning," Chloe stated.

Tamara shrugged.

"Neither did Roger," Tamara said. "Do you know that even if you don't know about a law and you break it, you'll still get charged? Our justice system is totally fucked up."

"They told me it was a party," Chloe said.

"Oh and it was. One helluva party," Tamara said.

"It was Patrick's idea," Shawn said.

"Dick. It was yours," Patrick shot back.

"Boys, boys, you're both guilty." Tamara said. She did a pull up on the metal bar. It seemed effortless.

"Tamara, that's not the point. The point is that what happened after, well, what happened was terrible. And wrong. It was inexcusable."

Tamara let her body go slack and fall back down to earth.

"Not interested in excuses. First time my dad did what bad dads do, he blamed alcohol. Grief over mom. I don't fall for that shit anymore," Tamara said cryptically.

"So, what can we do, Tamara? How can we make this up?" Chloe asked.

Tamara did five more pull-ups.

"Hmmm. When it's time for you to know, I'll tell you." And then she left the shadows of bleachers and walked towards the parking lot.

The five watched her go.

"What the hell did that mean?" Kisha asked.

Patrick punched Shawn hard in the arm.

"My idea?"

"Shut up," Shawn said and punched him back.

"She's gonna kill us," Kisha said.

"Not us," Jesse said. "Chloe and I were nice to her. Maybe she just wants to put all of this behind her."

"Uh did you not just hear her? She doesn't care who was actually responsible," Kisha said. "We're all in the same boat."

The football team was starting their practice on the other side of the bleachers and Shawn couldn't help but watch them warm up and stretch.

"That used to be me," he said with a twinge of sadness. Jesse listened to him and posited an idea.

"It's like you're looking at something you used to be, isn't it?"

Shawn shrugged.

Chloe understood where Jesse was going. "Tamara used to be dead and now she's alive."

"She's not dead," Patrick said. "Right?"

"Patrick, you said she might be a witch. Now I don't believe in any of that," Chloe said, "But something off. She's not herself anymore. She's like a new and improved Tamara. Strong. She shed twenty pounds in a day. And that confidence."

"Not to mention she literally rose from the grave," Jesse added.

"What are you saying?" Shawn asked.

"We go back to the woods," Chloe said.

Patrick blanched, "Are you crazy?"

"I'm not going near that place again. No way." Shawn said.

"You don't make decisions for the group. You started this. Your last brilliant idea, bury Tamara, didn't turn out so well." Chloe said. "So, we go back to the woods and make sure we're all not fucking crazy. Make sure the body is gone."

"She's right," Kisha said. "Sorry, babe. I need to see for myself."

After finally convincing Shawn, the kids left the bleachers. As they did, they didn't notice Bill warming up his car and watching them walk across the field.

Chapter 13

Dusk had set and a slight fog had overtaken the atmosphere of the woods. The last rays of the sun peeked in through the tall trees, dappling them with hints of gold. But the dense canopy of the forest quickly hid the shining. Vague animal noises emanated from the hidden corners of the thicket.

"Fuck this place," Patrick said. "I swear I hear a tiger."

"A tiger?" Kisha said.

"Whatever our version of that is," Patrick said.

"Just shut up and follow me," Chloe said, the de facto Magellan for this expedition. A branch snapped and Shawn jumped.

"Pussy," Patrick said.

"At least I know it's not a damn tiger," Shawn shot back.

Chloe ignored the bickering. "It's right up here," she said, pointing to a small clearing. Jesse grabbed Chloe's hand. Kisha once again bit her nails. Shawn wrapped his arms around her.

"Guys," Kisha said. "What if her body is still there?"

Chloe pushed through some shrubs. The edges of which made minor cuts in the her exposed skin.

"It's here," Chloe said. "This is where she was."

The patch of ground had definitely been disturbed. Dirt had shifted. Jesse kicked the ground.

Chloe bent down and began to dig. After a few minutes, she stated what was very obvious. "It's empty."

"There's blood everywhere, and Tamara's jacket and that lame lipstick she was wearing," Kisha said.

"God. She dug herself out," Chloe said.

"Why didn't she suffocate?" Jesse asked.

"Thank God she didn't," Chloe said. "She was never dead in the first place. I knew it."

A gust of wind blew heavy through the trees and Chloe turned to look. The darkness in the trees seemed menacing now. Threatening. Chloe glanced down to Tamara's grave and a scream caught in her throat. She saw the same thing she saw in her nightmare. Tamara's face in the shallow grave. Decayed. Worms and bugs nesting in the sockets that used to hold her sad eyes.

"She's here. Tamara. She's here," Chloe said.

"What's wrong?" Jesse asked. Chloe pointed to the grave.

"She's there," Chloe said. "I can see her!"

The others looked at Chloe, looked at the grave, looked around.

"It's empty. She's not here," Jesse said.

"I saw her. I swear," Chloe said.

"Aren't you supposed to be the normal one?" Patrick said.

Jesse grabbed Chloe and held her close. "I'm here." He looked Chloe directly in the eyes, and those two simple words meant the world to her.

"She's gone," Jesse said. He guided her down to the hole and she opened her eyes. She took a deep breath. Nothing was there.

"Sorry guys. I think I'm losing my mind," Chloe said.

Kisha walked behind her. "Don't apologize. This whole thing is just fucked."

As Chloe stood up, with Jesse's arms still wrapped around her, something caught her eye. A small piece of parchment. She reached into the dirt and grabbed it.

"What's that?" Shawn asked.

"Dunno," Chloe said.

Shawn grabbed it. "It's covered in blood. Can't read it."

"It's a fucking spell," Patrick said. He grabbed it from Shawn. "Yup. Same parchment. Same writing. My mom had tons of these things. Witch-bullshit. It ruined her life."

"Cocaine ruined her life, dude, " Shawn said, instantly regretting his words.

Suddenly, wind whipped through the trees. The loose dirt surrounding the open grave blew skyward in a typhoon of dust. Leaves came from nowhere and swirled amid the dirt.

And then it happened. A scream. Piercing. It was Tamara's scream. Everyone froze in fear. Until finally Shawn spoke.

"Let's get the hell out of here.

"Now," Patrick said.

Chapter 14

The willow tree in front of Mr. Natolly's house billowed in the blustering wind. Bill, framed by the bay window, stepped out from the hall into the kitchen, wearing a terry-cloth robe and boxers. He carried a glass of red wine and watched the branches outside sway in the maelstrom. After a few moments he went to the living room, sat down on the couch and, rested his head back, taking a sip of the wine. He closed his eyes, trying to forget Roger and the day.

"Can I have a sip?" A voice asked.

"Honey, we have Luna on the way," he said with his eyes still closed.

"What a memorable name. It's either gonna carry her far or destroy her."

Bill opened his eyes and standing in front of him, wearing her mother's red fuck- me-gown, was Tamara. The black dress had been nice, but this was pure sin.

Bill set the glass of wine down on the table, but did so clumsily, and a splash of it found its way out of the side of glass.

"Bill, you need to be more careful. That glass almost broke. Tamara moved towards the glass and wiped off the spilt liquid with her finger. Then she put her finger in her mouth and licked off the wine.

"What are you doing here?" Bill said.

Tamara climbed over him and sat down by his side.

"The door was unlocked and I needed to talk to someone," she said.

"Well, Allison's still at school. Talking with other students."

"I can wait for her to come back. Roger's death cut me deep." Tamara inched closer to Bill on the couch.

"I don't think this is a good idea." Bill said quietly.

"Like your robe," Tamara said, ignoring him. "You like my dress?"

Bill got up from the sofa.

"Mr. Natolly, I've been through so much lately. Roger. My father. My mother." She played the part of the grieving child to Shirley Temple perfection. Bill acquiesced and sat back down. But he made sure his robe was closed tight.

"Okay. Allison should be home soon. She can help."

"I know I shouldn't bring this up again, Mr. Natolly, but I've been thinking about what happened between us." She inched nearer to him on the sofa, as he inched away.

"We talked about this. Nothing happened," he said, and he reached for the wine glass. "I'm so sorry I misled you. I felt for you. I want you to be happy."

"Did you mislead me?"

Tamara took the wine glass from his hand and took a gulp.

"Look at me, Bill."

Bill didn't look. He turned the other cheek and tried to focus on something else.

"I said look at me."

"It was a mistake, Tamara."

She put the wine glass near his mouth and forced his mouth open. She poured in a mouthful.

"It was a mistake," he said as he swallowed, his eyes now closed.

"I'll ask you one more time to look at me."

Bill opened his eyes and did as she asked. His breathing became heavy.

"It's getting wet."

"What?" Bill asked stunned.

Tamara glanced down at the table. The glass of wine was leaving a wet ring. Tamara smiled innocently. Then she took the glass of wine. "I'll finish this for you." She let the glass linger on her lips and took a slow sip. "My dad guzzles. But I nurse." She ran her fingers through her hair. "You like my new look?"

"I liked your old look," he said.

"Don't patronize me. I'm not pathetic like she was." She took another drink and then leaned to him and forced open his mouth and streamed the wine from her mouth into his. "She was weak. I'm not. You felt sorry for her."

Bill wiped his lips, cleaning up the wine that had found its way down his chin. "I never felt sorry for you. I championed you."

Tamara's face hardened. She thought of the article, of how this all started. The life she led. The torment she endured. "No one liked me the way I was."

"It doesn't matter. You shouldn't change to try and please people, Tamara"

"For an English teacher you use a lot of really tired clichés."

Tamara took one more swill of wine. "I changed to please myself." She stood and lifted up her skirt. "Actually I changed because I wanted other people to please me." She lifted her skirt higher, showing her upper thighs, "Any idea how I can get someone to please me, teach?"

She put his hands on her ass and forced him to rub. Then she forced his hands to massage up and down her legs. "Any ideas coming to you now?"

She leaned in and kissed him. He kissed back. For a moment.

Then he stopped.

"I can't, Tamara."

"You will," she said, kissing his neck. Then, she bit it. She found his ass and grabbed it.

"Tamara, you have to go."

"No I don't," she said in a doll's voice.

"Yes you do."

Bill pushed her away and wrapped up his robe, hiding his dick.

"I love my wife," he said like one says a morning mantra.

Tamara looked into his eyes. Bill didn't match her stare.

"You have to go," he said.

"Well aren't you the loyal one?" Tamara grabbed Bill's crotch. Felt its hardness. "I know you want me. I can feel how much." She laughed, let him go, and then walked out the front door into the windy night.

Chapter 15

The next day at Sebastian High, the pallor of Roger's death loomed large. The monitors on the walls had been turned off. The students walked down the hallway in silent bustling. When the bell rang, they moved into their classes, relieved for a new day to begin. Relived to put some time and space between them and the horror they had seen yesterday.

Tamara had no desire to enter any classroom. She wore tight jeans and a halter-top, reminiscent of some 1980s hair band vixen. She walked to the guidance counselor's office and didn't even knock.

Allison was on the phone when Tamara entered.

"Knock, knock," Tamara said.

Allison put up her finger to indicate she was almost finished.

"Checkup tomorrow? Thanks Nurse Stevens. See you then," Allison said, then she hung up the phone. "Tamara, I'm so sorry I missed you last night." She had let her blonde hair fall down in errant strands that framed her face, giving her a look of maternal kindness.

"Don't worry, Mr. Natolly took really good care of me last night. At your house."

Allison was clearly taken aback by Tamara's comment and her tone. But she kept her cool.

"Tamara, that's an interesting outfit."

"It's hot, isn't it? I wanted to be cool." Tamara said and shimmied a bit to show off her clothes. "You like it?"

"Let's talk about you," Allison said, trying to focus.

"Great. Let's talk. I'd love to be analyzed," Tamara said.

Allison's phone rang, but she put it on silent.

"The doctor?"

"My mother."

Tamara smiled.

"How are you doing? About Roger's death?"

"It was sort of tremendous. The shock of it. The creativity of it," Tamara said. "What's your mother like?"

"Uh, she's fine. Tamara I need you to focus on what I'm saying."

"I am. Roger's death has got me thinking about what's really important. Like true love. Family. Mothers."

Allison reached over the desk and grabbed Tamara's hand.

"Honey, you're a teenager. You have time for all that. Your whole life."

"Roger doesn't."

"You're not Roger. And you need to understand the conflicting emotions, and feelings, you're going to experience because of the trauma you witnessed. You'll want to avoid it. But you need to let yourself walk through your feelings, no matter how painful. That's how you heal."

"I don't feel anything," Tamara said coldly.

"You're in shock. But when that passes, if you start feeling depressed, let me know. And focus on school. Your education. Mr. Natolly said you're an incredibly gifted young woman. Ivy League gifted. Having that sort of future can change your life."

"Are you saying my life needs changes?"

"Tamara, I'm saying you have the whole world in front of you and things are going to get better. I promise."

"That's easy for you to say. Not to be rude, but you have a steady job, a perfect husband."

"And you can have all those things too," Allison said, trying to sound as sincere as possible.

"Maybe. But I know there are no guarantees in life, and you know that too."

Allison felt a wave of quiet fear overcome her, as if Tamara was reading her thoughts, knew her insecurities. She maintained her composure.

"Events like what happened yesterday can inspire fear. It makes sense for you to be pondering these big ideas."

"Pondering?"

"You're thinking like a young woman who just witnessed a suicide."

Tamara fiddled with her halter-top. She scooted up in her chair. She nodded.

"Allison, I'm actually just afraid that I'm going to end up being 35 with nothing to look forward to but the slow march towards death and irrelevancy. Wait. That's your age, right?"

Allison laughed. "Next month."

Tamara didn't laugh. She stared right at Allison.

"So, thirty-five in a month and in a marriage you think is perfect, but isn't." Tamara said.

Allison tensed, but tried to keep her cool. "Tamara, that's not appropriate - -"

"I mean, what if I'm thirty-five and I think I need to get a better nose? A new face. A better ass. Anything that will make my man stay and not pull a Roger, figuratively of course. Us women get old and men just stay hot. It's so unfair."

"Why am I feeling you're more worried about this than I am?" Allison asked. Tamara sat still. She looked out the window.

"Tamara?"

"I'm sorry. Like you said, I'm being inappropriate. But, I can't stop wondering, if a woman can't give her husband what he needs, would it be his fault if he pulled the plug?"

"You're seventeen," Allison said. "There's no need for you to worry about anything like that."

Tamara laughed.

"So sweet. You think I'm worried about me?" Tamara rose from her chair and leaned over the desk and stroked Allison's fair,

Irish skin. Allison smiled and pulled away. She picked up her phone, even though no one had called.

"Tamara, I have an appointment I need to get to. But come back anytime."

Tamara turned to leave the office, but stopped at the door.

"Just to be clear, I don't do personal diatribes. Like a good book, the meaning, the really profound stuff, is found between the lines."

Allison didn't respond.

"You're thirty-five and you need work done. That face? Not good enough and won't age well. Bill will never stay." Tamara opened the door and then turned around again. "Oh, and you'll never give him a child. And we both know that's what he really wants, isn't it?"

Allison's face turned pale, then she dropped her phone and grabbed her stomach.

*

Mr. Natolly finished wiping his dry erase board as the door to his classroom flung open and before he turned around, slammed shut.

"It sounds like you and Tamara have gotten really close lately. Is that why she's acting so funny? Dressing up like a tramp."

"Allison?"

"I just spoke with Tamara, Bill."

Bill walked over to his wife. He grabbed her by her shoulders and pulled her into him. "And this is upsetting you, why?" he asked.

"She said you took good care of her last night. Was she at our house?" Allison waited for an answer and when it didn't come, she knew the answer. "What the hell was she doing at our house, Bill?"

"Whoa. Tamara came by looking for you. She was upset about Roger and thought you'd be home."

Allison pushed him off of her.

"Why didn't you tell me?"

"I didn't think it was important."

Allison's face flushed red. "And how did she know we had trouble conceiving?"

"Honey, I don't know what you're talking about."

"How many private conversations have you had with her?"

"Allison, why are you so upset? She's just a student. A sad, lonely student."

"She used to be, Bill. Not anymore. And she was talking to me like," Allison stopped. She put her hand near her mouth and whispered the rest of her thought. "Like something happened last night."

"Allison, that's ridiculous."

"I hope so. I hope I'm being a hormonal bitch," she said, as she began to tap her nails against her desk, which was clearly her go-to angry tic.

"Allison, you and Luna are all that matter to me." He reached over to grab her hand. Allison moved away. "Tamara is just in trauma mode," Bill said. "That's it. The whole school is in trauma mode."

Allison nodded her head and then walked out of Bill's classroom.

Chapter 16

Patrick strolled through the packed cafeteria. He went to each of the tables and passed out a flyer to every kid.

"What's this?" a shy freshman still in braces asked.

"Dude, like you need to ask?" Patrick responded.

The guy next to brace-face punched him in the shoulder.

"It's Patrickpalooza," the guy whispered. The kid with braces nodded, pretending to understand.

"Five. Patrickpalooza Five," Patrick corrected. "It's the only time I associate with freshman. Well, freshman guys," he said, as he spied something two tables over, or rather, two someones.

He left the kids in awe, then moved on, bypassing Chloe and Jesse who were at the next table, to what he really wanted. Two gorgeous freshmen, dipping fries in ranch.

"Girls," Patrick said. "be sure to get all that sauce in your mouth." The two girls giggled at his lame entendre. He gave them flyers for his party, gathering up as much charm as he could in the process. They took the flyers, then ignored him. Patrick moved on to the next table, where Kisha and Shawn were eating.

"I love freshmen," Patrick said. "So pure on the outside, but inside, they're begging for it."

"You're an ass," Kisha said bluntly.

"As long as I'm getting ass," he shot back. He looked down at Kisha's lunch. It was maybe an ounce of kale and a banana.

"What are you? A monkey?" Patrick said. "Eat something, girl."

"Was that racist?" Kisha asked.

Patrick quickly shook his head. "Monkeys aren't racist. Are they?"

"Idiot," Kisha said, glancing at the flyer in his hand. "I don't think I'm going. Not feeling very festive," she said.

Patrick put a flyer on her lap and let his hand linger on her thigh.

"Watch it," Shawn said. Patrick ignored him.

"I can't believe you're letting that freak get to you. I'm not letting that bitch ruin my senior year," Patrick said.

"Which one?" Kisha said, playing with her green plate of nothing food.

"Atta girl! Bite back! Shawn, you're with me, right bro?" Patrick said with pep.

Shawn took the flyer off Kisha's lap. He studied it like a map. Then he nodded.

"Totally in. Fuck Tamara."

*

Across the cafeteria the freshman kid with braces was studying the flyer. As he did, a hand reached down and snatched it from him. It was Tamara's. She now had her turn to study Patrick's Photoshopped flyer of half-naked clowns jumping into a swimming pool.

"He wants a circus?" Tamara said. "I'll give him the greatest show on earth."

Chloe and Jesse overheard Tamara. And they also saw an evil smile wrap around her face as she crumpled the flyer and put in the freshman's container of milk.

"I just lost my appetite," Chloe said, and pushed her burger away.

Chapter 17

Tamara stood near her locker rummaging through her bag.

"Tamara," a voice boomed out. She turned to it.

"Hey Bill," she said in a honeyed voice.

"My classroom. Now."

She gave him a look that let him know she liked his forceful tone. Then she closed her locker and zipped up her bag.

Bill watched her with steely eyes. Motioned for her to follow him.

They reached his classroom and once he had closed the door, Tamara said, "I love this alpha male routine."

"How do you know about the problems with my wife?"

Tamara put her hand to heart and feigned shock.

"You two are having problems?"

"Don't play games with me. How do you know? What's come over you? What did you say to her?"

"Enough with the barrage of questions. Relax. Just words, like literature. A collection of words was all I said to her."

"What did you tell her?"

"The truth. It's obvious she can't give you what you want, or need." Tamara said.

"I have everything I need."

"Keep telling yourself that and maybe you'll believe it. But deep down, in places you don't like to think exist, you know you'll never get what you really need from that boring bitch of a wife."

Bill lifted his hand to slap her. He held back.

"Do it. You'll love it and I'll love it."

Bill lowered his hand. "This…whatever you think it is, will never happen. Ever. I'm happy with my life, my wife. Everything."

Tamara slinked towards him.

"Stay away," he warned.

"Oh, Bill."

She reached out to touch his face. To start taking control of him. But, like his almost slap, she pulled back.

"Not yet," she said. Bill contorted his face, not sure of what she meant.

"Not ever," he said awkwardly, then watched as Tamara slowly left the classroom.

*

Chloe walked down the hall, still trying her best to avoid the mounted TV monitors that lined the walls. Roger's demise, she thought, might sting forever. She noticed the janitor fixing the broken glass trophy case. And then she heard a door slam. It was Mr. Natolly's classroom door and the slammer was Tamara. Chloe froze. Thankfully, Tamara walked the other direction.

Chloe walked towards Mr. Natolly's door and peeked in through the window. He was sitting as his desk, his head in his hands, maybe crying.

A hand clamped down on Chloe's shoulder. She spun around and was relieved it was Jesse. He smiled meekly. "Sorry, didn't mean to scare ya."

Chloe nodded at Mr. Natolly through the window. "Something's going on with him and Tamara," Chloe said.

"You think he's screwing her."

"Jesse!"

"Well, she is hot," Jessie said, "And crazy. Guys dig that."

Chloe shook her head, "Maybe high school boys. But he doesn't exactly look happy."

"True," Jesse replied. "I say you and I agree to just avoid her at all cost." Chloe nodded. "And on that note," he added, "I don't think we should go to Patrick's party."

"I thought you lived for big parties?"

"Not anymore."

Chloe paused. Then she reached in her bag and pulled out Patrick's flyer. "Tamara wasn't invited, but she saw this. She'll be there. I know it. What if she hurts someone?"

"That's not our problem," Jesse said.

"Everything that's happened since that night is our problem."

Jesse put a hand on her shoulder. "I just think we should just stay—"

"No. Shawn, Patrick, Kisha. They're all going to be there. If she's going, she's planning something. And I want to be there to confront her."

"Confront her? With what?"

"I have an idea about why this is all happening," Chloe started to say. But before she could finish, a loud crash echoed through the halls. The janitor had dropped a large pane of glass as he repaired the trophy case.

"Damn," the gray haired man said, looking at the shattered mess.

"Okay," Jesse said, as he turned back towards Chloe. "We'll go."

The two walked down the hall, hand in hand.

*

Bill's head was still in his hands when his door opened. He looked up. It was Allison.

"Thank God it's you," he said.

"Hon," she said in a forlorn voice.

"I don't know what's going on anymore," he said, missing the context clues on his wife's face that said something was terribly wrong.

"Hon," she said again.

"A decade at this school and the kids just get worse and worse."

"Bill." Finally he looked up. Her face was crestfallen, swollen from tears, dark streaks of runaway mascara lined her cheeks. "I went to the doctor today. And got the same news I get every time."

Bill's face filled with shock. He got up from his desk and went to her. He pulled her in to his chest and held her tight.

"Oh Ally. Ally. It's okay. We'll try again."

"I don't know if I can. I'm getting too exhausted to keep trying, and failing, at the one thing I want to succeed at the most," she said.

Chapter 18

As dusk fell on Crossmore Avenue, Tamara examined herself in the vanity.

"God, I love this," she said to her new, beautiful face. She bent down and slipped on heels. The door opened and her father entered.

"What do you want Mr. Riley?" Tamara asked, not taking her gaze off her own reflected image.

"Mr. Riley? How about Dad?"

"Titles need to be earned," she said as she modeled the heels, impressed with the inches of elevation.

He took a drink from his beer. "What does that mean?"

"Doesn't matter. What do you want?" Tamara did a hair shake to add body to her raven's coif.

"Just to tell you that you look beautiful."

Tamara took a final look in the mirror, seemed satisfied and walked to the door.

"What -- no hug for your old man?" he asked with a stupid grin.

Tamara stopped a foot from him. She could smell the booze and the body odor.

"You'd like a hug wouldn't you? Like having your hands on me?"

"For affection, honey. You and I? We're all we have." He put out his arms to have her come into them. "You're my girl."

"You're right, Dad," Tamara said. She leaned in to kiss him. She sensed his excitement at this, but just before the embrace took hold, she pulled back and took her hand and brushed his cheek with it.

And then images became ingrained in her father's eyes. His daughter's face, rotted and molding. Then a stripper, some sad fatherless girl dancing on a dirty stage. Then the image shifted out of the strip club, and onto a suburban street. A woman, who looked like a slightly altered version of Tamara, same black hair and green eyes, but with longer legs and fuller lips, walked into the small house on Crossmore and found her husband, fucking the drugged up stripper on the new leather sofa she'd worked doubles at the restaurant to pay for. A child's voice screamed, "Mommy!"

Then the images stopped for Mr. Riley. He opened his eyes. They had the same vacant stare that Roger's eyes had.

"And those were just a few of the better memories. I could have showed you a thousand more."

He nodded. "A thousand more."

"If you loved mom as much as the bottle, or the strippers or even me, we wouldn't be in this position, would we?"

He shook his head. "We wouldn't be in this position."

"You've done bad things, haven't you?"

He nodded again.

"Bet you'd like a drink now wouldn't you? Take the edge off?"

He nodded.

"I mean trying to screw your own daughter, well, that deserves a nice cold one."

"Honey, I would never do that to you."

"So you're calling me a liar?"

Her father seemed confused by the double-edged question.

"Dad, come on, follow me." Tamara said. He nodded. "Let's go to the kitchen," Tamara said. He walked down the stairs as if she was dragging him by a leash.

"Open the fridge," she commanded.

He did and grabbed a bottle of beer.

"That's what you really love isn't it? Not mom or me or the Chicago Bulls."

He nodded. "This is what I love."

"Then love it now."

Mr. Riley twisted off the cap and drew the bottle to his mouth. He took a sip and then set it down on the counter.

"Daddy, not like that. Love it the way you love everything else. Devour it."

He nodded. Then lifted the glass back up and bit into the bottle, as easily as if it was a ham sandwich. He chewed the glass. Blood gushed as the shards dug deep in to his tongue and mouth.

"That's it, Daddy."

He nodded and took another bite.

"Slow down. You've got plenty more."

Mr. Riley mindlessly set the broken bottle down, ignoring the crimson river pouring down his chin. He reached into the fridge, grabbed another bottle, and bit into with what was left of his broken teeth.

Chapter 19

Patrick's minor McMansion was packed with used cars, a few bikes, and tons of kids. Feral teens did beer bongs on the front lawn. A girl with dyed pink hair puked on the side of the road. The living room window was broken with a loud smash, followed by uproarious laughter from the idiot who'd fallen though. The party was officially on.

Inside, dance music reverberated through the house, drowning out the din from the revelers who were so drunk that every little word seemed funny or profound or recklessly perfect.

Shawn and Kisha stood in the corner, nursing beers. They watched three girls twerk up against three guys.

"Idiots," Kisha said.

"It's sorta hot," Shawn said.

"Never gonna happen," she snapped back. Shawn nodded to Patrick, who had entered the living room from the kitchen. He had three drinks placed strategically in his hands, and brought them to the two freshman girls he'd met earlier in the cafeteria.

"I have to applaud his game, babe," Shawn said. Kisha nodded and Shawn left her so that he could hover over Patrick as he worked the girls.

"Ladies," he said. "I'm the king. Welcome to my manor!"

They giggled. It was obvious they'd already had a few too many.

"Brought these for you. Special drinks for my special court members."

"I'm totally buzzed. I need to wait," one of the girls said. The other nodded and added, "Those last drinks were, like, really strong."

Patrick smiled like a cat about to get a canary.

"Girls. I told you. I'm the king. You do what the king asks. Drink up. I'll take care of you. That's what I do for my subjects."

The girls looked at each other. They took two drinks, leaving Patrick the third. He raised the cup, the girls toasted, then all three downed half the drink in one swill.

"Good little princesses!" Patrick said, and cupped both girls around their waists.

Shawn simply shook his head. Patrick turned to him.

"That's how you do it, buddy," Patrick said with a devilish grin.

Suddenly, the front door opened Patrick and Shawn's faces paled.

Tamara strolled into the house like she owned it.

Patrick shook his head in disbelief. Then went to stop her at the pass.

"This is a private party," he said, holding out his arm like a traffic cop.

Tamara looked around at the scores of people.

"I can tell it's very exclusive. Not like your quaint little hotel party."

Patrick winced. Tamara reached for him.

"Don't touch me," he said. But she did. She touched his cheek. Patrick's eyes turned black and he saw things he didn't want to see. The first thing he saw was what Roger and Tamara's dad had seen. Tamara's decayed face, pruned like an apple doll. It was monstrous. He tried to turn away, but he couldn't.

Then Tamara's visage disappeared and was replaced by an image of him adding a few drops of a clear liquid in to a drink. Then he heard the pounding of a bed backboard and the muffled protests of a girl, after consuming his altered drink, begging him to stop as he pushed into her. He saw blood from a male's fingernails on her back and shoulders. Then the images stopped and Patrick stood in erect repose, staring blankly at Tamara.

"Thanks for coming," he said to her. "I love that dress. Let's get you a drink." His voice had genteel quality to it. He took Tamara's hand and guided her across the room. They passed Kisha and Shawn.

"What the hell?" Kisha asked.

Patrick led Tamara to the two young freshman girls.

Like Shawn had done earlier, they both inched closer to Patrick and his harem. Trying their best to interlope.

"Hello my little princesses. This is Tamara. She's our queen."

The two girls didn't know what to say. They each took a sip of their drinks.

"Put those drinks down girls," Tamara said. "And Patrick, go get me something. Without roofies." Patrick hesitated. "Now," Tamara said.

Patrick nodded and left.

"He was such a douche to us. But you have him whipped," one of the girls said.

Tamara sighed. "God, you two are so stupid you don't even deserve names. I'm just gonna call you Teen Whore One and Teen Whore Two," Tamara said to the girls, who were both still drinking. "I told you to put those drinks down."

The girls set the drinks down.

"How did you make him do that?" Teen Whore One said.

"Do what?"

"Stop trying to fuck us and go get you a drink?"

"Magic," Tamara said.

"You're amazing," Teen Whore Two said.

"I know. Now, go find a jock and work your own magic."

The girls nodded and left, in total awe. Tamara walked towards the kitchen, where Patrick was pouring her drink.

*

Chloe and Jesse entered from the backyard, both holding red cups containing only Sprite, not vodka. They'd made a choice to be cognizant and sober. They saw Kisha and Shawn hovering near Tamara and the newly dubbed teen whores, just before the small cabal disbanded.

"How's the party?" Jesse asked Kisha.

"Been here maybe an hour. Same old shit. Drunk and dumb," Kisha said.

"Remember when that used to be a great thing?" Shawn lamented.

"So. Tamara?" Chloe asked.

"She's up to something. She used her voodoo mind control on Patrick. He's acting weird," Kisha said.

"Guys," Chloe said. "I have to show you something."

She pulled out the bloody spell parchment that she found at Tamara's grave.

"Patrick may have been right," Chloe said. "About Tamara being—"

"Why the hell would you bring that?" Shawn asked.

"This spell has to have something to do with how she's changed. I know it sounds crazy. But we have to start accepting that there's more going on here than Tamara being a bitch. We need to confront her with this," Chloe said, holding up the paper. "Here, where there's a lot of people."

"Safety in numbers," Kisha said.

Chloe nodded.

"And then what?" Shawn asked.

"I don't know. But she's fucking with Mr. Natolly too. So she's not just after us. We have to stop her. We started this and we have to end it."

"Guys," Jesse said. "Shut it!"

Pure instinct prompted Chloe to stuff the parchment into her pocket.

"How sweet. All of my friends are here!" Tamara said. "All my besties!"

The kids stood rooted in silence.

"This place is off the hook!" Tamara said. "Music is great. Crowd is great. Life is great."

Patrick came over with a drink in his hand and gave it to Tamara. She took it and swirled the straw around.

"Not really much of a drinker," she said. "Patrick, why don't you take it?"

He looked at her lovingly, then took the drink and chugged the entire thing.

"Well, we're off. You guys have fun. I'll see each of you again. Soon. In the meantime, let loose. Have fun. This party should be killer."

Chloe and Kisha made awkward eye contact. Jesse and Shawn couldn't take their eyes off Tamara as she led Patrick in to the middle of the living room. A new pop song blared and Tamara began to dance, swaying seductively to the music. Patrick gulped another drink, threw the cup over his shoulder, then bodied up against Tamara. She ran her hands over her perfect curves. Then she allowed Patrick to do the same.

"Wanna dance, Clo?" Jesse asked, shamefully turned on by what he was seeing on the dance floor.

"You're joking." Chloe said.

Jesse blanched. "'Course I was."

Chloe rolled her eyes, just as Kisha pulled her close to her.

"I need to go use the bathroom," Kisha said.

"So go. Upstairs I'm sure," Chloe said, still watching Tamara and Patrick grind.

Kisha bit her nails. "I have a little problem. And I forgot to bring the one thing I need to solve it."

Chloe understood. "I'll come with. I have an extra one in my purse."

"You're a lifesaver."

"What are you two girls talking about?" Shawn asked.

Jesses shook his head. Smiled at Chloe. "You two go be girls. Shawn and I'll watch out for Tamara," he said. Chloe nodded and then she and Kisha walked through the crowd of swaying kids and up the stairs.

*

Jesse sipped his Sprite and looked around, bored. But not Shawn. He was fixated on Tamara and Patrick.

"I can't believe this shit," Shawn said.

"Shawn. Let it go. Until we know what we're up against, just drop it."

"I don't let things go, " Shawn said as he left Jesse standing alone and marched over to the dancing couple. He grabbed Patrick and turned him around.

"What are you doing, man?" Shawn said to Patrick.

Patrick's eyes were matte and empty. He said nothing; he just continued to dance badly. He acted as if Shawn wasn't there. Shawn turned back to Tamara.

"What did you do to him?"

"Just tackled him."

"Huh?" Shawn asked.

She reached up and touched his Shawn's face.

"Not all tackles involve helmets and shoulder pads," she said.

Shawn's eyes turned black. The party evaporated and all Shawn saw was the skeletal, skinless face of Tamara. Then he saw a needle being injected into his arm. He saw sores on his dick and heard himself lying to Kisha about them. He saw himself mounting an unconscious girl, as Patrick stood behind him, taking pictures. Then the images stopped. Shawn started to dance with Tamara and Patrick.

Tamara moved between them. She rubbed up and down. Patrick and Shawn got more and more into it. They grabbed at her like frenzied piranhas. At one point, Tamara stopped, looked across the room, and saw Jesse. She winked at him.

Both Shawn and Patrick tried to kiss her, but she stopped them.

However, she teased and grinded and groped. Both boys were crazy in lust.

And then the song ended. Tamara sighed.

"Well, looks like we have to find a new place to party boys."

They nodded. She whispered into each of their ears and they nodded again, this time more impassioned. Then Tamara took the boy's hands, left the dance floor and led them upstairs.

At the landing of the staircase, Tamara looked down at Jesse. Her cold eyes chilled him. Jesse turned away. And when he looked back, the three of them were out of sight.

"She's amazing," one of the newly minted teen whores said. "The football captain and the bad boy? Who gets both?"

"Some girls have all the luck," her friend said.

Jesse found some vodka and poured it into his Sprite.

Chapter 20

Tamara led the two boys into the last room in the long hall. She could hear the music from down below. She could hear the squeaks of the guy's sneakers emanating off the hardwood floor and she could hear the perfect silence of her total control over everything else.

She opened the bedroom door. It smelled like gym socks and unwashed boys. It smelled like Patrick. The room had all the normal stuff: bed, dresser, computer, headphones, Xbox console, general upheaval. Having surveyed the scene, she finally spoke.

"Come on in boys. It's time to have some fun," she said, crossing over the threshold. She then turned around and motioned the two to enter the room.

Patrick came in first, followed closely by Shawn.

"Shut the door Shawn," she said. He did.

Tamara went first to Patrick, slid her arms around his waist and kissed him.

"Been waiting for that for so long," he said to her.

"And you got it." She pushed him back onto the bed. He laughed as he fell onto the mattress and tried to pull her down with him, but he failed.

"Your turn," she said to Shawn. She beckoned him over. And as Patrick watched, Shawn grabbed her ass. She smacked his hand away. Then she pushed him onto the bed, next to Patrick.

Both of the guys began playing with their dicks through their pants, looking up at Tamara, who loomed above them.

"You want me, don't you?"

They both said yes, their teenage hormones raging, proved emphatically by the rise in their pants.

"More than those girls you fucked in the Jackson Hotel?" she asked.

They nodded again.

"The girls who were too drunk, or drugged, to say no?"

They nodded. Neither noticed that Tamara's seduction of them was officially over. She was now in attack mode. She reached down and stroked Patrick's leg.

"You know what would really turn me on?" she asked them both.

"What?" Shawn asked.

"For you to know what it if feels like to be used. Taken advantage of."

"That sounds hot," Shawn said.

Patrick agreed with a nod.

"Great," Tamara said, as she glared down at the boys, lying sprawled out on the bed. "So. Who's gonna pitch and who's gonna catch?"

She looked at the boys and pointed her finger at each of them, then alternated with each syllable.

"Eenie, Meenie, Miney, Moe?"

Her finger ended up on Patrick.

"And we have a winner. Turn over."

Patrick did as she asked. He stood up from the bed, then bent over it, spreading his hands wide on the bed for support. Shawn watched him do this, but didn't move.

"Shawn, you told me that night that my mouth wasn't good enough for your dick. But maybe Patrick's ass is. So, go ahead. Treat him like one of those drugged up girls."

Shawn rose up, still under Tamara's control, and grabbed Patrick by the hair. He violently yanked his head up, then down, like a rag doll.

"Tear the bitch's pants off."

Shawn reached around Patrick, who was still bent over the bed and unbuckled his jeans. He yanked them down. Patrick wore plaid boxers underneath.

"Good boy," Tamara said. Then she looked at Patrick. "You want it doggy style or missionary?"

Patrick didn't answer.

"Doggy it is. So, go ahead, Shawn. Give me a show. Oh, and we won't tell Patrick about the herpes. That will be our little secret," she said in a whisper.

Shawn shoved Patrick down hard. He tore a hole in the back of Patrick's boxers. Then he climbed on top of him. Shawn placed his elbow on the back of Patrick's neck. Pinning him down. Then he roughly thrust into him.

*

Jesse took another gulp from his newly spiked Sprite. A couple of junior girls leered at him but he ignored them. He checked his cell nervously.

Finally, Kisha and Chloe walked down the stairs.

"It's been, like, ten minutes. How long does that woman stuff take?"

"Long enough to know not to ask," Kisha said. Chloe looked around.

"Tamara?"

"I didn't know what to do. I don't even want to be here," he said defensively.

"Jesse?" Chloe said. "Where is she?"

"She took Patrick upstairs. And Shawn." Jesse said.

"Jesse!" Chloe said.

"I know, I froze. I've seen some crazy shit in LA, but nothing like her."

"Shawn's with her?" Kisha asked in a minor panic.

Jesse took another drink. "They both are. And they're acting weird. Like creatures from a bad zombie movie."

"You were supposed to watch her!" Chloe yelled.

"I did. I watched her walk up the stairs with two tranced-out puppy dogs."

Kisha knocked the drink out of Jesse's hand. Furious, she bee-lined it for the stairs. Jesse and Chloe were close behind her.

"Kisha!" Chloe yelled. "Stop."

"No, she may have gotten Roger and Patrick. But she isn't getting Shawn," Kisha said, putting her hand up, without turning around. Chloe and Jesse stopped following, unsure of what do.

Kisha raced up the stairs, down the hall, and pounded on Patrick's bedroom door. There was no answer, so she quit pounding and threw open the door.

Tamara stood just inside the room. Her arms crossed. Her lips curled.

"Where's Shawn?" Kisha screamed.

"Welcome to our private party," Tamara said. "And I think it's obvious where Shawn is."

Tamara stepped to the side, revealing Shawn raping Patrick on the bed. Shawn grunted with intensity. Patrick moaned in pain that now bordered on pleasure.

Kisha put her hand to her mouth in shock. Her eyes widened. She ran over to Shawn and tried to pry him off of Patrick, to no avail. "Stop it, Shawn! Stop!" But her pleas fell on deaf ears.

From down the hall, Chloe and Jesse, who had decided to come after Kisha, were nearing Patrick's room. Tamara lifted her hand and the door slammed shut, leaving Chloe and Jesse on the outside, unable to look in.

Kisha could hear Chloe's voice, on the other side of the door, begging her to get out of the room, but Kisha didn't listen. She quit trying to stop Shawn, but she couldn't leave.

"Kisha," Tamara said softly.

Kisha turned and found herself face to face with a set of green eyes.

"What did you do to them?" Kisha asked.

"Oh, come on. It's not like you didn't know he was screwing girls behind your back," Tamara said in a little girl's doll voice.

Kisha was paralyzed with fear. Tamara stepped closer to her.

"God, you have a beautiful face," Tamara said with a forlorn, dramatic sigh. And then she reached out and touched it.

Kisha's eyes turned black. She, like the others, saw images she'd rather never have seen. Maggots squirmed in Tamara's eyes and wormed their way through her temples, leaving divots of flesh in her face. Then Kisha saw images of blood and fat being sucked from a body. She saw herself gorging on food. Then huddled over a toilet, forcing herself to vomit.

Then the images stopped. Kisha came back to the present, but her eyes were dead and black, just like the others had been after Tamara's touch.

"I used to envy your beauty. Now I pity it. You're an embarrassment to women," Tamara said tauntingly as she circled around Kisha. "Bulimia? You've watched way too many Lifetime movies."

Tamara led Kisha to the mirror above Patrick's dresser. She rested her head on Kisha's shoulder, so they both could look at each other.

"You have a perfect body," Tamara said, and lifted Kisha's shirt to reveal her firm stomach. "Flawless skin," Tamara said, as she rubbed Kisha's stomach, letting her fingers linger around the navel. Then she let her hand leave the navel, trace her breasts, her gazelle like neck and then her face.

"But deep down, Kish? What do you see?"

Outside the room, Chloe was still pounding on the door with futile strain, trying to get it.

"Kisha!" Chloe screamed.

"God, will she ever shut up?" Tamara asked with a wry smile. "Ignore her, Kisha. Look at yourself. Deeply. And tell me. Who are you?"

Kisha stared at herself. She squinted her eyes. "I don't know," she said.

"I do. A girl so vain, so desperate to keep her asshole boyfriend, a boyfriend she won't even know in two years, that she'll do anything. Even if it means destroying herself from the inside out."

Kisha couldn't quit staring at herself in the mirror.

"Question. Does your man know what you do to make yourself prom queen ready?"

Kisha looked over at Shawn, who was still pounding away at Patrick. She shook her head.

"Maybe it's time to show him."

Kisha suddenly rammed her hand down her own throat and a stream of bile poured out. Green, vile, acidic emptiness in the form of projectile vomit. She couldn't stop doing it, even when there was no more bile left to regurgitate.

From outside the door, Chloe and Jesse heard the sounds of Kisha's vomiting as well as the guttural noises coming from Shawn and Patrick. She turned to Jesse, "What the hell's going on in there?" Jesse didn't answer. Instead, he slammed his shoulder in to the door, trying to break it down. But it was like hitting brick.

Inside the room, Kisha's vomit had now turned to blood. And then, somehow, her organs began to be purged. Bits of intestines came out of her, falling to the floor. She took a step and slipped on the blood and bile that had formed a puddle on the ground. She fell hard to the floor. Yet, she kept putting her hand down her throat, trying to find some semblance of beauty in the ugliness of her insides.

"You're never gonna find what you're looking for, Kisha," Tamara said, reading her thoughts.

Tamara bent down and touched Kisha's face again. Kisha stood up and everything returned to normal. The room was clean. No blood. No bile. Kisha looked at herself in the mirror and a sense of calm overtook her.

"Actually, you're skin and bones, Kisha. You really need to eat something."

Kisha nodded. She slowly walked to the door, ignoring the fact that her boyfriend was still raping his best friend. She opened the door, and closed it before Chloe and Jesse could see inside.

Kisha walked past the worried kids and started down the hall.

"Are you okay?" Chloe said, grabbing her arm.

"Fine." Kisha said without blinking an eye.

"We heard you scream," Jesse added.

"I'm starving."

Chloe released Kisha and turned to go back into the bedroom. She dug in her purse for the parchment that had Tamara's spell on it.

"I'm ending this now," Chloe said to Jesse.

She grabbed the doorknob. Couldn't get it to open.

"Fuck it," Chloe said, trying to convince herself she was changing her mind out of duty and not fear of Tamara, "We'll take care of Tamara later. Let's make sure Kisha's okay," Chloe said. She and Jesse went after her.

Jesse and Chloe found Kisha in the kitchen. She was devouring a slice of apple pie she'd pilfered from Patrick's fridge. Jesse and Chloe shared a quizzical look, but didn't say a word. After Kisha finished the pie, they watched as she found a bag of chips in the cupboard. She tore the bag open and shoveled down handfuls of chips. When she finished, she turned the bag upside down and emptied the crumbs into her mouth. Kisha tossed the empty bad aside, then moved on to a breaded chicken breast in a to-go container, some leftovers from a night out.

Finally, Chloe spoke up.

"Kish? What happened up there?"

Kisha ignored her. She continued to eat. She was now binging on cold pasta carbonara.

"We have to call Mr. Natolly," Chloe said to Jesse.

"Or the cops."

"And tell them what? We buried Tamara in the woods and now she's back and putting spells on us or something?" Chloe asked, pulling out the parchment.

"Well, when you put it like that."

"Get Kisha. We have to go," Chloe said. Jesse grabbed Kisha by the arm and started to push her towards the exit. Kisha grunted, grabbed a loose slice of ham and ate it like it was her last meal, then allowed herself to be led away by Jesse.

*

Outside Patrick's house, Chloe dialed 411 and asked the operator for William Natolly's number. The operator found it and patched Chloe through.

At the Natolly house, the phone rang. Allison was watching a Law and Order rerun. Bill, in usual boxers and robe, munched casually on microwave popcorn.

"You get it," Allison said, too upset to muster the necessary politeness a phone call would require. Tonight was her night to drink Scotch. Bill reached for the phone.

"Bill here," he said into the receiver.

He nodded. He nodded again, and then again. Then he hung up.

"What?" Allison said.

"I told you there was something going on with these kids. That was Chloe. Tamara's done something."

"What does that mean?" Allison asked, as he got up, found his jeans on the ground, and put them on.

"Chloe was vague, but she sounded terrified. I have to go. I'll be back soon." He leaned over and kissed her forehead.

"You're a teacher. It's not smart getting involved in students' personal lives. If they're having problems, call their parents. Or the police," Allison said.

"Normally I'd agree, but Tamara's already involved us."

"Fine. Just be careful," Allison said and she took a sip from her liquid cure.

Chapter 21

"Why are we meeting Natolly at 7-11?" Jesse asked, as he looked at himself in the passenger-side mirror of Chloe's hatch back.

"Kisha needs food," Chloe said.

"If you tell Mr. Natolly what happened, we could go to jail," Jesse said.

"Man up. Jail is what we deserve. And maybe it isn't the worst thing that could happen to us.

"So why call Natolly? If you want to get this over with, just call the cops already?"

"I already told you, I think he may be involved. Tamara is messing with him, just like us," Chloe said. "Maybe he can help us figure out what's going on so no one goes to jail. And then maybe we can all go back to being stupid high school students with our stupid high school problems."

In the backseat, Kisha was now devouring bean dip and Pringles.

"Mind if I go get a soda while we wait?" Jesse asked.

"I could use something, too." They both looked back at Kisha. She was like a wild animal that had found its prey. "We'll lock her in," Chloe said.

The moment Chloe and Jesse left for the neon lights of the market, Kisha put down her food. She took out her phone from her pocket. She called Shawn.

Back in Patrick's room, Tamara heard the phone ringing from Shawn's discarded pants and grabbed it.

"Hello. Shawn can't come to the phone right now, he's fucking Patrick." Tamara. said into the phone.

*

"Forgot, my wallet," Chloe said, as she and Jesse entered the store. "Be right back." She headed back for the car. As she opened the door she heard Kisha talking into her phone.

"Mr. Natolly is meeting them at the 7-11 on Wilmington Avenue. They're going to tell him everything."

Chloe grabbed the phone from Kisha and flung it out the door.

"What are you doing?" Chloe asked.

Jesse came running back to the car. "What happened?"

"She called Tamara."

"What? This is just great. Does she know where we are?"

"I don't know," Chloe said, looking Kisha, who continued to devour food. "But we need to keep things under control," Chloe said. "Kisha?"

"Hmm?" Kisha said in between bites of her chips.

"I have a plan to help Tamara."

Kisha paused for a moment and looked at Chloe. And as she did, Chloe punched her in the face, knocking her out cold.

"What the—?" Jesse said, looking at the slumped over Kisha.

"Take off you belt," Chloe said.

Jesse eyed Chloe incredulously. "Really? Now? Look, I think you're hot and all, but with all the stuff going down, I don't think I could even get it -- "

"Idiot. We need to tie her up. "

Jesse turned red. Tried to cover. "Of course. I knew that. I was just kidding." Chloe shot him an impatient look. Jesse took off his belt. Then he and Chloe reached into the back seat. Chloe grabbed Kisha hands, as Jesse wrapped the belt around her wrists. Suddenly, Chloe gasped in horror.

"Oh my God," Chloe said.

"What?" Jesse asked as he struggled with the belt.

"She wasn't just eating potato chips,' Chloe said. She lifted up Kisha's hands. The tips of her fingers had been gnawed on. Bits of flesh and fingernails were missing.

Jesse recoiled and tried to calm his heaving stomach. Chloe sucked in some courage and tied Kisha's hands to the door with the belt. She turned to Jesse. Saw that he was on the verge of throwing up. "I'm gonna get some stuff for her fingers," she said calmly. "Everything's going to be alright."

Jesse nodded as Chloe went back into the 7-11. But his eyes betrayed the fact that he didn't believe her.

*

Tamara paced back and forth in Patrick's room. Shawn was still plowing Patrick. "Get up. Get dressed. Change of plans," she ordered. "Now." The guys looked up at her and nodded.

Chapter 22

Bill pulled up next to Chloe's car, under the neon sheen of a liquor store. Both Bill and Chloe got out of their cars at the same time.

"What are you two doing out in the middle of the night?" Bill asked.

"It's like nine o'clock."

"I meant it's past school hours," Bill said to Jesse. "This better be good."

Jesse and Chloe looked at each. Chloe nervously bit her lower lip. Jesse stared at Bill for a long awkward moment.

"You can start any time now," Bill said. His voice stern.

Jesse looked at Chloe nervously. She straightened.

"Last weekend," Chloe started to say. Then she stopped.

"We were invited to a party," Jesse added, finishing her thought.

"It was Shawn's idea."

"And Patrick's. But mostly Shawn's."

"Kids. Slow down. So, you went to a party?"

Jesse and Chloe dropped their heads.

"It wasn't a party. We didn't know what it really was. We had no idea," Chloe pleaded.

"I think we need to go to Tamara's house," Jesse said. "She needs major help."

"I agree. But you have to tell me what happened at this party," Bill said.

The night chilled. Chloe filled Bill in on what had happened, as the clouds rolled across the nearly starless sky, hiding the moon and then showing it, then hiding it again.

She told him about the party. About burying Tamara. About her returning to school. And the spell. As Bill listened, a storm of emotions washed across his face. Shock. Disbelief. Anger.

Finally, Chloe finished. She and Jesse stood, waiting for a response from their stunned teacher.

Bill paced the parking lot. "This is crazy."

"That's what we thought," Chloe said. "But then Roger died. And the boys at the party. And now Kisha. Chloe nodded towards her car. Bill walked over. Glanced in the back seat and saw Kisha, tied and bound.

"Look at her hands," Chloe said cryptically. Bill did and saw that the tips of her fingers where bandaged with gauze. Gauze stained with blood.

"What the hell?" Bill asked.

"Tamara did something to her. She wouldn't stop eating. She chewed her own fingers," Chloe said.

"There's got to be a rational explanation. Drugs. Mass hysteria. Something. I don't believe in witchcraft," Bill said.

"I didn't either. But you tell me how Tamara leaves school on a Friday and then comes in on Monday looking like a supermodel."

Bill stood still. He was at a loss.

*

Allison was watching some banal soap opera and sipping her drink. She was doing her best to sink entirely into the sofa. Anything not to think of the fleeting memory of Luna. The volume of the TV was loud, but she barely heard the dramatic monologues spouted by the put upon mistress.

She also didn't hear what was going on outside of her house. Shawn and Patrick had shown up. With butcher knives. As the mistress on the television planned her revenge against her married lover's wife, Tamara's proxies were planning a similar fate for Allison.

*

Bill looked at Kisha, then to Chloe and Jesse. "Tamara's just a sad girl who was given nothing in life. She's not a witch. Witches don't exist," Bill said.

Chloe took out the parchment and handed it Bill.

"She's a witch. This is her blood. We spilled it and this spell brought her back. She won't stop until everyone who hurt her is dead," Chloe said emphatically.

Bill looked again at Kisha. "What happens if we let her loose?" he asked.

"She'll eat her arm off," Chloe said, with zero irony.

"We have to get her to the hospital," Bill said.

"She's fine. The bleeding's stopped," Chloe said. "We have to deal with Tamara first. Plus, if we let Kisha go, Tamara might summon her or something. Like she did the others."

"Others?" Bill asked.

"Shawn and Patrick," Jesse said. "It was like she had them hypnotized or something. They were following her around."

"How?"

Chloe shook her head and threw up her hands in mock defeat.

"However she's doing what she's doing," Jesse said.

"We thought she had you too," Chloe said.

"She doesn't," Bill said, almost defensively. But it was clear from his voice that he was worried. "Well, we can't just stand here doing nothing."

"I think we should call the cops," Chloe said.

"With your story? They'll just lock you up," Bill said, shaking his head. "Let's go talk to her father. Maybe he can clue us in on all of this."

"Great idea," Jesse said, happy that getting police involved was rejected.

"Let's go," Bill said. "I'll drive with you two. Well, you three," he said, nearly forgetting Kisha was present.

*

"Guys, let me handle this, okay?" Mr. Natolly said, as they pulled into Tamara's driveway.

"Deal," Jesse said. Chloe nodded in agreement.

"And both of you, make sure Kisha doesn't ... well, if she wakes up, make sure she doesn't eat herself."

Chloe and Jesse watched Bill walk across street, which was cluttered with litter, to Tamara's house on Crossmore Avenue. He knocked on the door. After a long moment he tried the door, it was unlocked. He disappeared into the dark abyss of Tamara's home.

"Whoa, Mr. Natolly, breaking and entering. My respect for the man just increased tenfold," Jesse said with a grin. Chloe glanced at him, "Do you ever take things seriously?"

Jesse glanced at Kisha's unconscious form in the back seat at the car. "One of my best friends had a heart attack when he was 15. Another one got hit by a car. The driver was sober. Her tire just blew and she lost control. Two deaths. No rhymn or reason. So, you ask me, life's just one big joke. And this shit, I mean, come on, we're talking about zombie witches, how can you not laugh."

Chloe took in what he was saying. Nodded slightly. "You're right. It does sound a little funny," she said as she turned towards to the house. "You know, Kisha's out cold. I think we should go make sure Mr. Natolly's okay."

She jumped out of the car and Jesse, reluctantly, followed her.

Bill crept through the living room like a burglar. His sighed as he took in the squalor that was Tamara's everyday life. Junk everywhere. Dilapidated walls decaying with chipped paint and excess mold. Holes dotted the ceiling. The obtuse smell of mice and mildew overwhelmed him. The house was worse than anything he'd imagined. A house full of unfinished deeds, broken goods, and damaged everything.

"Mr. Riley?" Bill said, as he walked through the chaos.

"Bill," a female voice said back.

He turned.

"Chloe?"

"We wanted to make sure you we alright."

"And find out what's going on," Jesse said.

"Okay," Bill said. "Let's see if Mr. Riley knows anything useful and then we'll get out of here."

The three walked through the first floor, past the blaring television, past the stairwell, and into the kitchen. Chloe screamed when she entered and saw Mr. Riley, bloody and slumped on the floor, surrounded by empty, and partially eaten, beer bottles.

"Mr. Riley!" Bill yelled, rushing over to him. He lifted Mr. Riley's head and blood poured from his throat. Bill tried his best to keep his voice soothing. "I'm Tamara's English teacher." Bill felt for a pulse and didn't find one.

Bill's features went slack. He turned to the kids and shook his head.

Suddenly, a noise emanated from somewhere in Mr. Riley's bowels.

"Mr. Natolly," Chloe warned. Bill stood up and backed away from Mr. Riley. Suddenly, the man's stomach began to expand. The button on his jeans popped open. His eyes opened and closed, then fluttered uncontrollably.

Everyone exchanged panicked looks. Unsure what was happening.

They got their answer when suddenly, after another deep groan of warning, Mr. Riley's stomach exploded, spraying the floor, counter and the kids with a fresh coat of innards.

"Oh shit, oh shit!" Jesse yelled, flinging blood and gore off him. "He just fucking detonated. Right now."

Chloe didn't freak out though. She deliberately wiped the blood off of her face and turned to Bill. "Now do you believe us?"

Bill nodded numbly, as he shook a bloody clump of Mr. Riley's stomach from his arm.

"What do we do," Jesse asked as he rushed to the filthy sink and tried to rinse off the rest of the crimson that stained him.

Chloe thought for a moment. Then she pulled out the parchment with the spell Tamara used on it. "Her father can't help us. But girls, we keep all of our secrets in our room."

"Well, let's go find hers," Bill said as they left the kitchen.

They moved through the dark house, bumping in to the corpses of old electronics that were spread everywhere as they crept upstairs and found Tamara's room. They opened the door, entered and began to rummage around.

"Man, it's even more depressing in here than downstairs," Jesse said. "Where's her boy band posters, or toys, or pictures?"

"We decorate our rooms with our dreams for the future," Chloe said as she took in the dark, sad room. "It looks like Tamara didn't have many."

"Well that's changed now," Jesse said. "She's definitely dreaming about killing us."

"Guys," Bill said, cutting off their conversation. He moved to Tamara's desk. Sitting on top of it was a red stained handkerchief.

"That's mine," Bill said He picked it up and then pointed to the hand-stitched BN on the upper right.

"A handkerchief? Really? Who still has those?" Jesse said.

"People not from LA. People who have class," Bill snapped.

"Oh yeah, a teacher in Hickville," Jesse sneered. "You're just oozing class."

Bill stepped up to him. "I don't want to hear another smartass remark from you. You did this."

"Enough," Chloe yelled. "Look."

The tone of her voice compelled Jesse and Bill to turn. She was touching a book on Tamara's dresser. An ornate book next to the rumpled pages of her first draft of the steroid article. It was Tamara's spell book.

Chloe picked up the book. Held it with a mixture of fear and curiosity. She traded looks with Jesse and Bill. Then she opened it.

Chapter 23

Allison was having her favorite dream. Fourth of July, fireworks, strawberry shortcake. A white picket-fenced place to raise a kid. America at its best. A crash woke her up. She was clutching Bill's pillow.

"Bill?" she said in that first daze of wakefulness.

But he wasn't there.

She looked at his side of the bed, then the clock. It was past midnight. She grabbed for the phone, concerned for him. She dialed his cell, but the call went straight to voicemail. She called a few more times. Her worry swelled with each unanswered call.

She instinctively felt her stomach. It took her a moment to realize Luna was gone. She pushed that painful memory aside. Her thoughts now all on Bill. Then she heard a creak downstairs. Allison rose nervously.

On the desk, just near her bed, she grabbed a letter opener. And even as she did it, she felt ridiculous. But it was sharp. And sharpness was something she felt she needed.

*

Bill, Chloe and Jesse stood in Tamara's room, the image of Mr. Riley's decimated body still in their minds. Chloe opened the spell book.

"There's a page torn out," she said.

"So?"

"It's the page I have. It has to be," Chloe said as she pulled the page from her pocket. She put it near the book and suddenly, the blood on the page started to fade away.

Chloe, Bill and Jesse started at the page, shocked as the blood evaporated and the previously crimson-soaked writing became visible. Their eyes scanned the page.

"It's a love spell," Chloe said in the night. "That's all it was." These words felt like empty vessels leading nowhere.

Jesse leaned in and read a passage. His brow furrowed. "A touch is what gives her the power," Jesse read.

Bill skimmed down the page, then he read: "Like this flame, my mother's flame. Let me rise like a Phoenix and reclaim all that is mine."

They paused.

"We did this. We created her," Chloe said. "We killed her and then brought her back." Then Chloe's face darkened. She turned to Bill. "And when it says she wants to claim what is hers, she's talking about you."

Bill shook his head in disbelief. "What?"

"Shawn told her she was meeting you at the hotel," Jesse said like a sad dog.

They all three looked at the spell book like looking at a nightmare realized.

*

Allison had fallen back asleep, but she kept the letter opener close. And like before, she woke up again. She took a few heavy breaths. She searched for her cell. She found it. She started to call Bill. But as she did, she saw a face flash before her.

It was Shawn. Standing in the bedroom door. But then the image went away. Nothing was there.

Allison sighed. She needed a drink. A glass of milk, she thought.

Still clutching the letter opener in her right hand, Alison sat up on the couch. She picked up the landline, which was on the table next to the couch and tried to call Bill again. She wanted to hear his voice.

But the phone line was dead. Or so she thought. Allison's eyes traced the route of the phone cord and her heart stopped when she saw the phone line had been cut. As her hands wrapped tighter around the letter opener, she saw something in the reflection of the living room window. It was Shawn. But his time, she knew it wasn't a dream. This time it was real.

"Shawn?"

She saw that Shawn held something in his hand. Something that gleaned. A knife.

He lunged for her as she tore up from the couch and ran down the hall. She kept telling herself it was all a bad dream. With each step. Bad dream. Step. Bad dream.

But she could hear his laughter behind her. She rounded a corner and slammed in to Patrick.

The letter opener dropped to the floor.

Mrs. Natolly, you're so jumpy. Aren't guidance counselors supposed to be all calm and collected.

"Patrick?" she said. Allison's heart pounded when she saw that Patrick was carrying a knife as well. A large, hunting knife. Allison glanced down at the letter opener, which was lying on the ground, dangerously out of reach.

"You remember me. That's good. You should. You and your husband held me back. You all never saw my potential."

Patrick advanced, forcing her into the living room.

"And your asshole husband ruined my life with that article," Shawn said from behind.

Allison turned to face him. Her wheels spinning.

"Why are here? Threatening me. I thought you hated Tamara," Allison said.

"Oh no. I hate everyone now," Shawn said.

Allison tried to keep her rising fear from showing. Tried to look calm as her mind screamed.

Patrick was in front of her, Shawn behind her, and they held those knives like swords. She saw them make eye contact and knew it was about to be over. She had one chance. She grabbed the first thing she could, a snow globe, a gift of her mother's from a trip to Iceland, and smashed it across Shawn's face so hard his jaw cracked. It worked. Shawn staggered back and Allison bolted for the basement, closed the door and locked it.

"Bitch," Shawn said, the blood that seeped from his mouth seemed to have no effect on him at all.

Patrick and Shawn rushed over and started to pound on the door. As they tried, Allison grabbed Bill's hammer from his work bench. He loved to build models of Pompeii. She hated how much he seemed to love dead thing; his classic books and Romantic poets. She also hated it when he asked if he could have this part of the house all to himself. As independent as she was, it made her feel apart from him. But now? She couldn't have been happier about his man cave.

Allison could hear them breaking down the door. She panicked. She saw the small window in the corner.

*

Bill tried calling Allison's phone. Again and again.

"Something's wrong," he said.

Let's get to her," Jesse said.

"Guys," Bill said. "This might not be safe."

"We're going with you," Chloe said.

"Mrs. Natolly was the first person I spoke to at Sebastian High. She was kind. It was cool," Jesse said.

Bill lowered his head, put two fingers on the bridge of his nose to stop from crying. Then he lifted his head back up and clapped his hands.

"Like Jesse said. Let's get to her."

*

Allison reached up and opened the window. She pushed herself up, using a small table, and tried to squeeze herself through it. But the table teetered. As Allison struggled to regain her balance, she could hear Patrick and Shawn pound against the door. She knew it had to be now or never. She jumped up and tried to pull herself through the window, but she slipped. The table toppled over and Allison fell from the window. She stumbled back and cut her foot on one of Bill's other projects: Luna's crib.

Behind her the door slammed opened.

Patrick and Shawn walked down the stairs. Knives in hand.

"Sorry. But Tamara wants you dead," Shawn said.

"Why?" Allison said as she lunged for the window again. But she could only manage to grab the bottom and peer out at the lawn above. And in that moment, she felt like Tamara. Stuck and trapped by nothing of her own fault.

"I barely even know her," she said meekly.

"That's the problem," Shawn said. "Oh, and you have the man she wants."

Patrick put out his left hand as if trying to calm Allison with it. "It's almost over. Just relax and take it," Patrick said, as they both descended upon her. But Allison had another idea. Next to the window, propped against the wall, was a snow shovel. Allison grabbed it and slammed it into Patrick, who was just a few steps ahead of Shawn.

Patrick fell back into Shawn, both their knives dropped. Before the boys could recover, Allison swung the shovel again and it clanged against Patrick's skull. He fell to his knees. Without hesitating, Allison arched the shovel through the air and slammed it against the side of Shawn's head. He dropped too. Allison screamed a primal scream and lifted the shovel. She hit them again, on the head, several times. Blood splattered the room with each blow of the snow shovel. The boys went still. Lifeless.

Allison calmed for a minute. But seeing the boy's bodies made her shake. Blood was everywhere. She dropped the shovel, ashamed of what she'd been forced to do. Then Allison shook off her shock long enough to realize she would have to step over the boys in order to escape the basement and get back upstairs.

Allison's body trembled as she leaned down and picked up the shovel again. She looked at the blood. Her mind reeled. Nothing felt right. Not the blood, not her stomach or the two boys she had just killed.

She slowly walked over Patrick, then Shawn, her nerves on edge. Just as she did and saw salvation in the stairs before her, the bloody boys both rose up like Lazarus. Shawn first. His head already a bloody mess. Allison smacked him with the shovel with all the force she could muster. Denting the side of his head. He took another step and Allison hit him again, so hard the end of the shovel broke. The metal flew across the room and Shawn fell back to the ground in a heap. Dead.

But Patrick was very much alive and grabbed her leg. Allison panicked as she fell to the cold floor. Patrick was on her in a flash. He grabbed her throat. Choked her.

Allison struggled for air. Her hand flailed and thankfully found the broken wooden shovel handle. With its jagged edge. As the world around her began to dim, Allison clutched the handle and rammed it up with all her might. The ragged edge smashed into the side of Patrick's head. The jagged edge punctured his skull.

His grip loosened. His mouth opened. Bloor rained down on Allison as Patrick hovered over her for a moment. Then he fell to the side and his body went still.

Allison quickly rose, rubbing her sore throat. Wiping the blood from her face. She raced up the stairs. Halted at the top to look back down the stairs at the fallen boys. Just to make sure they were dead. Then she spun around and ran into something. Or, someone.

Allison screamed.

"Mrs. Natolly?"

"I have to leave," she said to the stranger. And then noticed his blue uniform and his badge and, thankfully, his gun.

"Your husband called us."

"I have to go before the get up again. They're not human. I kept killing them and they wouldn't die."

"Who?" The cop asked.

Allison pointed down the steps of the basement. The cop peered through. Shawn and Patrick's dead bodies lay in heaps on the ground.

"Those boys aren't waking up, ma'am."

She fell into his arms.

Chapter 24

Bill and Chloe's car peeled into the parking lot of the Jackson hospital. It was late. The lot was almost empty. Bill parked in front of the emergency room. He opened his door and bolted to Chloe's car, which had stopped behind him.

As Chloe stepped out, Bill stopped her. "I got a call from the police. Allison's here."

"What," Chloe asked.

"Shawn and Patrick attacked her. But she's okay."

Bill said as he looked at Kisha in the back seat. "How's she?"

"Still out." Jesse responded, then he turned to Chloe. "You should be a boxer."

Bill opened the door and gently picked up Kisha's body.

"Careful," Chloe said.

Bill hurried through the ER door carrying Kisha, as Chloe and Jesse rushed behind him.

*

"What happened?" the doctor asked, as he looked at Kisha's hands. By now, two orderlies had laid Kisha on a gurney.

"We don't know," was all Bill could offer. He looked at Chloe and Jesse. "Guys, can you take care of this? I've gotta check on Allison."

"Of course," Chloe said.

As Bill rushed out to the reception area, the doctor checked Kisha's pulse and turned to a nurse. "Take her to Exam room three. Type and cross for two units of packed cells."

As Kisha was wheeled, off the doctor gave Chloe and Jesse a suspicious look and followed after his new patient.

*

Bill went back out front and asked the receptionist for his wife's room number.

"Her name?" she said.

"Allison Natolly."

"And you are?" The receptionist asked.

"Her husband."

"321."

"Thanks."

As he began to leave, Chloe and Jesse came out into the hall.

"They're running tests on Kisha," Jesse said.

"We want to make sure your wife's okay," Chloe added.

"Nope. Family only," the receptionist called after them. She filed her nails. "And I know you two ain't family."

"Thanks guys." Bill said. "I'll check on her and come back down. Go get something drink. And eat. You've been running around all night."

"There's a vending machine in the cafeteria down the hall," the receptionist said.

*

At the Natolly house, police cars abounded. The crime scene was attended to by all the usual suspects. Yellow tape, investigators, even German Shepherds.

Officer Haft, who was the cop who ran into Allison, sat on the porch smoking his first cigarette in fifteen years.

"Something wrong here?" a voice asked.

Officer Haft jumped up. He dropped his cigarette.

It was Tamara.

"Sorry, just been a rough night."

"Rough nights are, well, rough."

She put the cigarette back in his mouth. "Suck it up," she said, rubbing his face as she did.

"Where is she?" Tamara asked seductively.

"Who?"

"Don't make me ask again," she said without any seduction whatsoever.

Officer Haft took a deep hit off the smoke and then exhaled.

*

Bill rushed towards Allison's hospital room. A guard was waiting at the door.

"You are?" he said, his mustache some faded image from the 1970s.

"Her husband."

"ID?"

Bill showed it to him after digging it out from his wallet.

"Sorry. This was crime related. Want to make sure you're—"

"I'm her husband," he said with veracity.

The officer opened the door.

"Oh God," Bill said as he saw his wife, her wounds, her weakness.

"Bill?"

"Babe, I'm here."

He went to her and grabbed her hand, which was almost lifeless. He stroked her head.

"They said Tamara wanted me dead. And they had this soulless look in their eyes. And they were so strong. What's going on? How is she doing this? I mean, if it's her versus me, she'll win."

"No, she won't."

In a hardly audible whisper she said, "I killed them. I had to. Shawn. Patrick. It was me or them and I chose me."

"You chose us. You chose right."

He grabbed her hand and kissed it and then she fell asleep.

Chapter 25

Jesse and Chloe sat in the gloomy cafeteria. Behind them, a man, too old to even care about anything, cooked food that no one wanted to eat behind his closed little gate.

"This place is depressing as shit," Jesse said.

"Then it matches this whole week," Chloe said as she dug some money out of her pack and went to the vending machine.

*

Chloe's mother rushed into the ER, tears streaked her distraught face. She told the receptionist who she was and the receptionist quickly told her that Chloe wasn't a patient.

"Thank God. Where is she? Where's my baby?"

"Try the cafeteria."

*

Chloe chugged on a can of soda. Then turned to Jesse, who was drinking coffee and devouring a Twix bar. "We have to find her," Chloe said.

"Tamara?"

"No, Jesse. Hillary Clinton. Of course Tamara."

Jesse thought about this.

"I agree. But we need to wait for Bill. That's who she wants," Jesse said as he drank more of the stale coffee.

Suddenly he straightened.

"Your mom?" he asked, seeing Chloe's mother race down the hall. Chloe turned.

"Chloe!" her mother yelled. The two raced to each other and hugged tightly.

*

The doctor and nurse looked over Kisha's sedated body.

"Her BP is 110 over 60. No tox screen yet," the nurse said.

"That's well within normal range," the doctor said. "I guess we'll just have to wait for the lab results." The two left Kisha. As just the door shut, her eyes opened.

"She's here," Kisha said as if the rapture was beginning.

*

Tamara casually walked into the hospital. She went to the receptionist.

"Mrs. Natolly's room?"

"You aren't family? You can't go."

Tamara reached over and touched the receptionist's face. Her eyes turned black.

"Room number. Please."

"321. Elevator is right around the corner," the receptionist said.

"Thanks," Tamara said. "Oh, and sweet dreams."

The receptionist instantly slumped over, her face hit the desk hard as she fell asleep.

*

Kisha's eyes were wide open as Tamara entered her room. She rose up from her gurney.

"Glad you finally ate," Tamara said, noting her bloodied fingertips.

*

"Mom," was all Chloe could say, before she melted into her. "Nothing is making sense anymore."

"Like your poetry? Your little songs about sadness?" her mom replied with a cold laugh.

Jesse rose up from the bench. Chloe tensed in her mother's arm.

"Mom?"

"Sweetie, Tamara came over today. She told me that you don't like boys.

"What?" Chloe asked.

"I raised you right. Catholic. I dealt with your pixie haircut and bad rock bands. But girls?" her mom said. "After all we've done for you, you turn out to be a dyke?"

"Mom. Please!"

"You might as well have plunged a knife into my heart, Chloe."

"You don't mean that."

"I guess I'll return the favor." Chloe's mom reached into her purse and pulled out a butcher knife. Chloe and Jesse stood frozen as their brains tried to register what they were seeing.

Chloe's mother shook her head in disappointment. "One bad deed deserves another." Her mother, whose eyes were filled with rage, took a stab at Chloe. She barely managed to swerve out of the way, as the knife sliced her shirt. Jesse, jumped up and tried to wrestle the knife away from Mrs. Bowman, but she was strong. Too strong.

"Boy, let the women battle this out," she said. Then, as if Tamara had given her more strength than she ought to have, she smacked Jesse in the face and sent him flying across the room. He hit the vending machine so hard that he shattered the glass. The machine teetered and Mrs. Bowman tipped it over. It almost landed on the stunned Jesse, but her rolled out of the way in the nick of time.

"Mom, what the hell are you doing!" Chloe yelled.

"Just this." She kicked Jesse in the stomach. "Men always think they have to step in and save us. When they can't even save themselves." Another vicious punch doubled Jesse over and he cried out in agony.

Mrs. Bowman turned to Chloe. "And you? My little abomination of a daughter? You're next." Mrs. Bowman left Jesse down for the count and quickly descended on Chloe, her knife raised high. She began to furiously stab at Chloe. Chloe avoided the first blows. But then the blade hit its mark and sliced her arm. Then her shoulder. Blood poured out.

As Chloe saw another swipe of the deadly blade aim for her face, she dove to the ground. She grabbed some glass from the fallen vending machine. Spun towards her mother.

"Mom, please."

"I'm not your mother. Not anymore," Mrs. Bowman said in an icy tone. "And don't look at this as me killing you. I'm saving you from eternal damnation." She charged. Chloe, desperate and with a heavy heart, stabbed the glass shard in to her mother's leg.

But that didn't stop her. She brought the butcher down again, stabbing the hard floor right next to Chloe's head. Chloe arched up with the glass shard and jammed it in to her mother's side. Not deep enough to kill. But deep enough to wound. As her mother fell to the ground, Chloe grabbed her knife and pulled the stunned Jesse to his feet.

"You okay?" Chloe asked.

"Yeah. Are you?" Jesse said.

"No. I just got outed and stabbed my mom. I'm the opposite of okay," Chloe said.

"Those things your mother said, she didn't mean them," Jesse said.

"I'm not so sure."

"It's Tamara," Jesse insisted. "She's controlling her."

But Chloe was clearly stung to the core. She looked down at the blood from her mother's initial strike dripping from her arm.

"You'll be fine," Jesse said. He ripped off a piece of his shirt and used it as a tourniquet to slow the bleeding of Chloe's arm. "Luckily we're in a hospital."

Suddenly, Chloe tensed. "My mom, if Tamara got to her and is after Allison, then she's here too."

*

On the large elevator, going to the third floor, Jesse saw that Chloe was still reeling from the fight with her mother. He tried to lighten the mood. "I sort of I knew you were gay. I mean, who could resist me?" He asked with a Cheshire grin.

"Not the time for humor," Chloe said.

"Whatever. I'm just saying you're perfect the way you are."

Chloe smiled. And just as she leaned in to hug him, the elevator dinged and the door opened. The kids gasped. Kisha stood in the doorway, holding a scalpel.

Before the kids could move, Kisha, tried to slash Chloe. She missed once, then tried and hit the same place Chloe's mother did. Chloe fought back a scream. Jesse attacked Kisha. He smashed her across the face. It sent her reeling, back into the corner of the elevator. Chloe and Jesse leapt out of the elevator just as the doors closed, sealing Kisha inside.

"Fuck you," they heard her yell from the elevator.

"Run," Chloe said to Jesse as she heard the screech that signaled that Kisha had pulled the emergency stop button in the elevator.

And they did. They ran down the hall. Behind them, they heard the elevator open.

Chloe saw a stairwell up ahead. She pulled Jesse into it and the kids bolted down the stairs. Kisha was close on their heels. All three ran like banshees. But Chloe and Jesse beat Kisha. As Chloe and Jesse burst from the staircase, she scanned the area. Up ahead was the cafeteria. Chloe yanked Jesse toward it.

They charged through the door. Passed Chloe's mom and the smashed vending machine.

Jesse said, "What now?"

Chloe saw the double doors that led to the man cooking horrible food. She led Jesse there, just as Kisha was about to catch up with them. They locked the doors.

"Can't be back here," the man said. The kitchen was large and industrious and perfect for sick people at a hospital.

"This is life and death," Jesse said.

"Welcome to a hospital," the man said, unaffected.

Across the room, Kisha roared into the cafeteria. Fast. Determined.

"Listen, you need to leave. Things are about to get ugly," Jesse said.

The man saw Kisha, a blur or furry and rage approaching.

"My shift's over," the man said and hurried out the door.

As he left, Kisha began to pound on the locked double doors. Jesse grabbed a knife.

"This isn't her, Jesse. It's Tamara. We can't kill her. We've done enough damage already."

"It doesn't matter who started this. She's gonna kill us, Chloe," Jesse said.

Chloe looked around. She saw a freezer.

"Come on. Drop the knife," she said. Jesse put down the knife and Chloe picked up a large rolling pin.

"So, no stabbing. Just pounding with a rolling pin?" Jesse asked.

"Yeah, that's the idea," Chloe said as she and Jesse rushed to the freezer.

They opened the freezer and stepped in to the coldness, just as Kisha broke through the locked double doors. As they hid, they could hear Kisha stalking through the cafeteria.

"Ladies and gentlemen, I know there are at least two of you here," Kisha said, twirling the scalpel. "I don't mind trying to find you. I'm a cheerleader. I like games. But instead of playing with pom-poms...I'm going to play doctor. And see what your insides look like."

Kisha found the knife that Jesse left on the counter and she grabbed it.

She roamed around the kitchen. She opened the storage room.

"Damn," she yelled, when she found it empty.

She opened the dry goods room.

"Where are you two?" she yelled again.

Chloe and Jesse held each other in the freezer, as Kisha footsteps came closer and closer. Jesse took the rolling pin from Chloe.

"She's gonna find us," he said.

And then Kisha's voice and bravado disappeared. They heard her footsteps fade. After a long moment that felt like forever, Jesse turned to Chloe. "You think she's gone?"

"There's only one way to find out," Chloe said. Then she made a bold choice. She opened the freezer door. Scanned the area. It looked empty.

Chloe and Jesse inched out of the freezer. They made it several feet and halted. That's when they saw blood dropping from a rack of flour like small drips of honey.
The kids locked up and saw Kisha perched on top of the flour rack like some vicious gargoyle.

"Fooled you," Kisha said. The blood was remnants of her fingertips, which had started bleeding again. But her cunning was in full force, totally healthy.

She jumped down from the rack and went after Chloe first. She slammed her into the stainless steel oven. She went for her knife and was about to stab her. But before she could tear into her, Jesse took the rolling pin and smashed it into Kisha's back. She fell down and Jesse grabbed Chloe and pulled her out of harm's way.

Kisha started to rise. Jesse moved over to her and hit her over the head with rolling pin.

Kisha was hardly fazed. She grabbed a stainless steel cart that was laden with dry goods and pushed it at him, knocking him back.

"I was gonna start with Chloe, but I guess I'll start with you." She took her knife and stabbed Jesse in the gut. Twice.

Despite the pain lancing his body, he fought back and took the same cart and slammed it back into Kisha, causing her to drop the knife. He grabbed it.

"Kisha, I don't want to do this," he said. "Fight Tamara. Fight all of this."

Kisha smiled. "You're right. I should fight."

Then she a took frying pan that was next to her and slammed it into him, rendering him nearly unconscious. She grabbed him, turned on the oven that the union man had just been cooking bad eggs on, and put his face on it. She waited for it to heat up and burn him.

"Fighting and frying. Two similar words, often with the same results. Cooked shit," Kisha said.

As she did this, Chloe began to come to. She saw what was happening. And that Kisha, had dropped her scalpel. She grabbed it and lunged towards Kisha. But instead of stabbing her, she pulled down the dry storage unit. It fell on Kisha, knocking her to the ground. Pinning her.

Meanwhile Jesse came to, as the stove heated up. He pulled up quickly, and small piece of his skin sizzled on the hot stove. Jesse yelled and covered his wound.

Chloe bolted to him. She gently took his hand. "Let me see."

After hesitating for a long moment, Jesse removed his hand. A section of his temple and cheek were seared and scarred.

"How bad is it,?" he asked panicking. Chloe forced a smile.

"It didn't get too hot. It'll heal. You'll have a cool Sid Vicious thing going on."

"And what about her?" Jesse asked, watching Kisha writhe under the weight of the flour and margarine.

They both looked at the walk-in freezer.

Chapter 26

"Bill, there's no way can this be magic," Allison said.

"You haven't seen what I saw. And what about Shawn and Patrick? They suddenly became two violent murderers overnight?"

Outside, down the hall, they heard the guard talking to someone. Bill rushed over and peeked out the door. The blood ran from his face. Hallway down the hall, the guard had confronted Tamara. He held out his hand. "Sorry miss, you can't be on this floor."

Bill rushed over to Allison. His face was made of pure horror. "We have to leave. Now."

Bill didn't give his wife time to question or protest. He helped her out of her hospital bed. Her feet, still bandaged and bloodied, stopped her from moving quickly.

"I know it's going to hurt, but if you have to, can you run?"

Allison was confused, but nodded. As they headed to the door, both Bill and Allison heard Tamara in the hallway say "Let me touch your face."

"That's how she does it," Bill said. "Come on."

Bill and Allison rushed through the door. They caught sight of Tamara touching the guard's face. He stiffened. Under her control. Bill started to lead Allison down the hall in the opposite direction. Tamara saw them.

"Hello, lover," she said to Bill.

"Allison, run!" Bill said. They both rushed away from Tamara. Allison's feet bled through the bandages leaving footprints of crimson with every step. Tamara oddly didn't bother to chase after them. She just walked slowly, as if knowing their capture was predestined.

*

Jesse put a broom on the door handle of the freezer, locking Kisha, who raved like mad, in the cooler.

"Time for Tamara," Chloe said.

"Let's get her," Jesse said. But as he did, as they started to walk out of the kitchen, Jesse fell. In his own blood. It poured down his legs from the two deep wounds where Kisha stabbed him.

"No," Chloe said.

"She got me. She got me good. I was so high on adrenaline, I didn't realize it." He tried to sit up on the tile. There was blood everywhere. Too much blood.

"Wait, I'll go and get a doctor."

"No. Stay. Please. Don't leave me."

"I have to get help."

"It's too late," Jesse said, his voice wavering. "But listen, did I ever tell you why I moved here?"

She shook her head as tears welled up in her eyes.

"I hated LA. I wanted something simple. I wanted something kind. So do me two favors?"

She nodded.

"Be you. Please be you. Be kind, be simple."

"What does that mean?"

"Find a nice girl. Make her as happy as you've made me."

She nodded. The tears now flowed down her face.

"It was never you, Jesse."

"I know. And what happened, none of this, was your fault, Chloe. Promise me you won't blame yourself."

His eyes started to roll back in his head.

"Jesse, oh my God."

"I was gonna write a rock opera. I was gonna do lots of things, but you know what? I met you and that made this all worthwhile."

"Jesse—"

"And stop that bitch. Stop Tamara. That will be my rock opera."

And then he closed his eyes and the last bit of life drained from him. Chloe leaned in and kissed his forehead and then let out a primal scream of absolute rage, not unlike Tamara's, way back at the Jackson Hotel.

*

Bill and Allison rushed down the hallway, knowing full well that Tamara and the guard were after them. They kept looking behind and watching as Tamara methodically stalked them. They turned a corner. And ran into Chloe's mother.

"Mr. Natolly," she said. It was obvious that she was under Tamara's control. "You're looking not so well."

Allison pointed to the stairwell.

As the two of them entered the small maze of the stairwell, they realized that this wasn't a normal stairwell. The stairs didn't lead down, only up.

"Damn. This is roof access only," Bill said.

*

Chloe left the kitchen, left Jesse, left Kisha. Her spirit was broken. For the first time she felt like Tamara must have felt before all this happened. Hopeless. She took the elevator to the third floor. She wandered the halls a bit. Then, she slouched down, exhausted, and as she did she noticed a fire extinguisher. And beside it, encased in glass, a fire axe. Chloe grabbed a fire extinguisher and broke the glass to get the fire axe. Then she pulled the fire alarm. She knew she needed backup. Then she walked slowly down the hall.

*

Bill and Allison reached the roof. Dashed to the edge. There was no ladder. No escape. They looked down at the ground below and the cement and the five-flight jump.

"It might be better," Allison said. She once again grabbed her belly. "It just might be better."

"I will not let her hurt you."

"She already has. She took our child."

Allison looked out at the stars that were sprinkling the sky. None of that magic seemed to matter to her now.

Then, the door of the roof entrance opened.

Tamara, the guard, and Mrs. Bowman walked through.

As the three approached, Allison found new resolve.

"He loves me, Tamara. He loves me and not you and I'm sorry for that."

Tamara laughed.

"You can't give him a kid. How simple is that? I mean there are TV shows about teen moms, and you can't give your husband one damn baby?"

Allison let her head fall, for just a bit.

Tamara nodded to the guard who grabbed Bill. He tried to fight back, he swung, but he was no match. Then Chloe's mother grabbed Allison.

"Bill, do you know the sacrifice I made for you?" Tamara said. "Do you know what I did for you? I died for you."

As Chloe's mom held on to Allison like a vice grip, she couldn't help but respond.

"I'd die for him too," Allison said. Mrs. Bowman slapped Allison across the face.

"Oh, that can be arranged," Tamara said. She nodded to the guard again. He took out his gun. Pointed it at Allison. He was about to shoot, when from out of nowhere, his hand went missing.

Everyone was stunned to see Chloe on the roof, wielding the fire axe. Her face was hard and cold as she turned to Tamara.

"You did die in that hotel room that night. I get you had it rough, but now you're a monster." Chloe swung the axe at Tamara, and hit her right in the stomach. The force flung Tamara back to the ground. But she quickly got up, the axe still protruding from her stomach.

"I did die. And yet, here I am. And guess what? I can't die twice." She pulled the axe from her stomach and the deep gash magically healed itself. Then Tamara punched Chloe in the face, sending her reeling back, almost off the edge of the roof.

The guard picked up the gun with his intact hand and aimed it at Allison.

"Do it," Tamara commanded, and then she advanced on Chloe.

"Chloe, run," Bill said.

They all knew this meant that Bill and Allison didn't have a chance. They were both as good as dead.

"I'm not running," Chloe said.

"How sweet Chloe. And since you have so much hubris and charm, I'm gonna give you a taste of what you really want. A thrill before you die." Tamara walked up to her. Chloe backed away, but her mother pushed her back into Tamara's arms. This time, Tamara didn't just touch her face, she kissed her. Hard.

Like Roger and the others, images smashed through Chloe's mind. But these weren't like the other ones that Tamara saw.

Tamara saw Chloe defend her in the locker room. Chloe tell Kisha to give Tamara a chance. Chloe mortified when she saw what Shawn had done to her back at the Jackson Hotel. Chloe telling all of them, Kisha, Jesse, Shawn, Roger, and Patrick that they had to call the police.

Tamara pulled away from Chloe's face, ending the kiss. Tamara looked at if she'd just been scalded by boiling water. Her face contorted. Her fingers twitched. She almost looked as if she felt remorse.

"No," Tamara said, and took both of her hands and rubbed them up and down Chloe's face. But it didn't work. Chloe was still herself.

"You'll do what I say," Tamara said. She rubbed her hands again. Then again. "You'll do what I say."

And then it worked.

"I'll do what you say, Tamara," Chloe said. Tamara smiled her wicked smile and then whispered in her ear. Chloe picked up the axe and went towards Allison. She pushed aside her mother, who, also under Tamara's spell, was happy to oblige. The guard still had his gun pointed at Bill.

"Bill," Allison said with a woman's plea.

"Chloe, no. No," Bill said.

But her eyes had glazed over and she had the axe raised and ready to strike. At Allison.

"Tamara, stop this," Bill said.

"Stop what, lover? Making our destiny finally happen?"

Bill walked to the ledge of the roof.

"If Chloe hurts Allison I jump."

Tamara could tell he was serious. She waved her hands and Chloe put down the axe.

"Swear to God, Tamara," Bill threatened.

"God? I've been dead. All that exists after death is darkness."

He stood on the edge.

"This isn't you. The girl I was so fond of understood pain and beauty and all the things that lie in between. She never fought for evil. She fought for good despite the fact that there is so much evil in the world," Bill said, as he stood on the ledge, inching closer to the edge.

And with those words Tamara began to sob. Her beauty faded. She turned back to her old, homely self.

"Duality," she said. "Jekyll and Hyde."

Chloe and her mother stared at her. Allison was concerned with her husband so close to the edge.

"Not dichotomy. I chose to be a monster."

"You wanted love, Tamara, and you'll get it. But you can't control people to get it," Bill said.

"All I had to do was touch you and you would have been mine."

"But you didn't. You made the right choice," Allison said.

Tamara began to fade away. She continued to revert back to her old self. He acne returned, her thin face got full again, her hair became wisps of thin darkness.

"I killed everyone. I'm Frankenstein's creature. Not Jane Eyre. But I least I let you be real, Bill. I let you try and love me for me, not because of my power."

Bill stepped away from the ledge. As he did, he noticed that not only had Tamara turned back into her old self, she was decaying. Her face began to melt. It turned skeletal. Her death was back.

"It's okay, we can help you," Bill said.

Her decaying flesh worsened. She looked more and more like a corpse. She glanced down and saw what was happening to her body. Her eyes narrowed.

"No. I won't die again. I can't," she said. She looked up at him, and her ravaging beauty returned. Bill looked over at Allison. She nodded. And then at Chloe, who was in a trance. And he made the choice, the only choice he could make.

"Come here, Tamara," he said. "If you want me, you can have me."

Tamara froze. Not believing him. "Don't lie to me. I've been lied to my whole life."

"I'm not lying," Bill insisted. "If you want to be with me, if that will make you happy, then we'll be together."

Tamara was shaken by this prospect. Sure, she'd dreamed about it for years, but the reality of being with Bill was almost too much to handle. "Really?" she whispered.

"Really," Bill said with outstretched hands. "Come here. Kiss me and I'll prove it."

Tamara practically beamed as she went to Bill and melted in his arms. They kissed. And Tamara finally had the one thing in life she wanted. But after a few moments of this passionate kiss, Bill's grip tightened around Tamara. And as everyone watched in horror, he hurled himself and Tamara off the edge of the roof. Tamara screamed as she realized what was happening. But her screams were cut short when she and Bill slammed into the concrete below. More blood shed. Allison screamed. But her scream couldn't save Bill from a five-story fall. She looked over the edge of the roof and saw his twisted body below.

Everyone on the roof, who was under Tamara's control returned to their normal selves. Confused about how they got there and what happened.

*

"He saved us," Chloe said, as she and Allison and her mother looked down at the two broken bodies. "She bound them together and he did the only he could to stop her."

Allison sobbed. She tried to stop, but couldn't.

Chapter 27

Police cars swarmed the crime scene. Chloe, Allison, the guard, and Mrs. Bowman all were treated for their various wounds. Doctors and nurses told each of them how lucky they were to be alive, but they knew that. Allison and Chloe had the hardest time.

"The only man I ever loved," Allison told Chloe.

Chloe nodded. She knew there was nothing she could say to quell Allison's anguish. She just reached out and put a comforting arm around her. The women sat in silence trying to comprehend all they'd been through.

*

Kisha had escaped from her frozen cell. The old man had come back to the kitchen to get some soup for a prickly old patient and found her trapped there. She blamed it on too much Vicodin and a propensity for sleepwalking.

"Go lie down, girl," he told her.

"I will," she said.

"And the broom stick in the door?"

"I'm not well. What can I say?"

He laughed. "Want some soup?"

"Not hungry," she said and left him in the kitchen, Jesse's body unseen in the corner.

She walked down the halls of the hospital. She left the receptionist at her desk. She walked more and saw Chloe and the others being treated. She looked at her bandaged fingertips and smiled. She went outside, saw the remnants of Tamara and Bill on the ground, but didn't give them a second thought. Tamara was still in Bill's arms, a tangled mess of sadness. The police were out and in full force and didn't notice her.

She found Bill's car. She opened the passenger-side door and picked up the spell book that Chloe had taken from Tamara's house. She thumbed through it and came upon a spell called Resurrection and Immortality. She smiled. Cradled the book in her arms. She closed the door of the car and walked off into the night.

ACKNOWLEDGMENTS

This book would not have come to fruition without the help, and support, of numerous friends, colleagues and family. We would like to thank the following people: Michael Roman (the cover rocks), Chela Johnson, Lionsgate, Jenna Dewan, the cast and crew of Tamara, Steve Nunez, Angela Anderson, Martin Aguilera, Eef Fontanez, Stephen Zimmer, Jeff Locker, John Stancari, Brad Stocking, Alan Wethern, Bill Halfon, Katie Disabato, Luke Shanahan, Gene Stone, Millicent Rovello, Emily Root, Kathy Myers, Amy Doyle, and Laura Spencer. And an extra, extra thanks to Paul Bellaff.

Dedicated to Elizabeth Reddick, Shaina Reddick and Linda Doyle.

ABOUT THE AUTHORS

Jeffrey Reddick is a screenwriter, best know for creating the "Final Destination" film franchise. Jeffrey attended Berea College and currently resides in Los Angeles.

J.D. Matthews is a novelist and screenwriter. He attended Loyola Marymount University and currently resides in Los Angeles.